MARY CAUGHT SIGHT OF THE SPLASH OUT OF THE CORNER OF HER EYE.

She heard the little girl scream a split second later. The girl had plunged into the water perilously close to the rocks and the dangerous tide that swirled past them—a tide that could carry the child out to sea or drag her down in a minute.

Mary snatched up her walkie-talkie.

"Mayday! Mayday!" she cried.

Mary raced down the beach, her eyes never leaving the stricken girl in the water.

Debbie was kicking and screaming. Mary suspected the girl knew how to swim, but the tide was too strong for her to struggle against it for long.

"I'm coming," Mary called. "Don't panic!"

But the girl was nearly finished. Debbie's kicks were growing weaker, and her screams had turned to racking sobs and gasps for air.

Mary knew it was now or never.

7th Heaven™

MARY'S RESCUE

by Amanda Christie

An Original Novel

Based on the hit TV series
created by Brenda Hampton

Random House New York

Published in the United States by
Random House Children's Books,
a division of Random House, Inc., New York,
and simultaneously in Canada
by Random House of Canada Limited, Toronto.

www.randomhouse.com/teens

Library of Congress Control Number: 2002116208
ISBN: 0-375-82409-X

Printed in the United States of America
First Edition
10 9 8 7 6 5 4 3 2 1

7th Heaven™

MARY'S RESCUE

ONE

"A lifeguard? At a beach town? For a whole month!"

Reverend Camden opened his mouth to speak again, but Mrs. Camden placed her index finger over Reverend Camden's lips, silencing him. She gave her husband a look that said he should stay quiet.

She doubted he would.

"You can't stop me, Dad," Mary said, tossing a stack of T-shirts into her suitcase. "I'm an adult."

"Barely an adult," Reverend Camden countered. "Practically not an adult. You certainly don't always behave like an adult, do you?"

"Well, the law says I'm an adult," Mary shot back. "I'm twenty-two years old."

She yanked open a drawer and pulled out more clothes, tossing them onto a growing pile on the bed.

"Even the law can be . . . in error," replied Reverend Camden. "Once in a while the law can even be wrong . . . sometimes."

"See!" Mary cried, closing the drawer with her hip and throwing up her hands. "That's why I'm going away for the month. All I did was come home for a day to pick up some extra clothes, and you're on me to change my plans."

"Not change them, necessarily," Reverend Camden said. "Just rethink them a little. When you said you had a month off from the airline, we were all hoping you would spend at least some of that time with the family."

"I'm an adult, and I want to be in a place where people treat me like one," Mary replied. "And obviously that's not here. So I'm going to be a lifeguard at Pacific Paradise!"

Mary pushed her hair back into place and took a deep breath. She didn't want to start yelling, but her father made her so mad sometimes.

"Dad," she said calmly. "I have a job. Responsibilities. People who trust me to do the right thing."

"They only trust you because they don't know—"

"Eric!" Mrs. Camden shot her husband a stern look. Reverend Camden's mouth snapped shut. When he opened it again, his words were spoken slowly and chosen more carefully.

"Mary," he said evenly. "You already have a job. A great job. You're a flight attendant, remember? Now, your family . . . Well, we all love you dearly. We want to spend some time with you before you go and . . . fly off into the stratosphere again."

"I'm a flight attendant with a month's vacation," Mary said. "So it's not likely I'll go flying off to the stratosphere anytime soon. And working as a lifeguard is a chance for me to earn some extra money."

Mary continued to pack her beach gear. She dumped the pile of clothes into her suitcase. Then tried to close it. The suitcase was so stuffed with clothes that it wouldn't lock.

She punched the clothes down and tried again. Still no luck.

"Since I don't go back to work for the airline until September," Mary continued, "I feel the need to do something constructive for the rest of the summer. When has either of you ever objected to work?"

"Never!" Mrs. Camden and her husband said in unison.

"Of course we understand," Reverend Camden said. "But couldn't you do something constructive around *here*? Somewhere within the city limits of Glenoak?"

"Like what?" Mary demanded. "Baby-sit the twins? I've been a baby-sitter . . . for Simon, for Ruthie . . . for the twins. I could be a waitress, but no one will hire me around here because they all hired me before and then fired me."

Mary paused, then shook her head.

"No, Dad. Now I want to do something else. Something more important."

"But do you have to go all the way up the coast?" Reverend Camden asked.

"Pacific Paradise is hardly all the way up the coast," Mary replied. "It's only a two-hour drive."

Mary hopped onto her suitcase to close it. Then, still sitting on it, she reached down and snapped the latches in place.

"I seem to remember the drive to Pacific Paradise takes closer to three hours," Reverend Camden said suspiciously. "Are you going to speed in Robbie's car? I don't think he would like that."

Mary's eyes flashed.

"Robbie wouldn't have lent me his car while he's out of town if he thought I would be speeding in it," Mary cried. "Robbie trusts me. Why can't you?"

"Calm down, Eric," Mrs. Camden said, jumping into the conversation. "Mary's right."

Reverend Camden's eyes widened in surprise. He was sure Annie would agree with *him*.

"But—" he stammered.

"Remember your heart condition," said Mrs. Camden.

"But—"

Mrs. Camden shot him a look, then turned to Mary.

"I think working as a lifeguard is a wonderful idea," she said. "And a job at

Pacific Paradise is a golden opportunity. You can earn some extra money before you go back to work at Jet Blue and maybe meet some interesting people."

Mary grinned. "That's what I said."

Mrs. Camden patted Mary's arm. "And you're right, sweetheart," she said, smiling.

"What are you thinking?" Reverend Camden asked. "A summer alone at a beach resort? There's bound to be parties and guys and who knows what else. It's a golden opportunity for trouble!" Mary and Mrs. Camden both glared at him.

Reverend Camden stood in the center of Mary's old bedroom, shaking his head in disbelief.

"I can't be hearing this," he muttered.

"Out!" Mrs. Camden said, pushing her husband to the door. "Let's give Mary privacy to pack her things."

"But—"

"You can help me make lunch, and we'll all eat together as a family one last time before Mary has to leave."

Mary smiled. "Thanks, Mom," she said, hugging Mrs. Camden. "Thanks for trusting me to do the right thing."

"I do, I do," she said, hugging back.

"And don't worry about your father's paranoia. He'll come around."

"I'll finish packing and come down for lunch," said Mary. "Then I'll get on the road."

"But—"

"Come on, Eric," Mrs. Camden ordered. "You were going to help me make lunch, remember?"

Then she turned to Mary. "Lunch in half an hour."

Still surprised that Annie was going along with Mary's insane scheme, Reverend Camden allowed himself to be led away.

But when she opened the door, it was Mrs. Camden's turn to be surprised.

As soon as she turned the knob, the door flew open and Simon and Lucy spilled into the room and onto the floor. They had been leaning against the door to eavesdrop on the conversation.

Ruthie was standing in the doorway, leaning against the wall. She shook her head in disgust.

"Amateurs!" she snorted, making a face. "Nobody uses that old door trick but complete amateurs."

"We were wondering what all the

shouting was about, that's all!" Lucy cried defensively as she jumped to her feet.

"Nobody was shouting," Mrs. Camden replied.

Ruthie spoke up. "I disagree. Dad was clearly shouting. I could hear him in my room. He interrupted my reading."

"I wasn't shouting," Reverend Camden insisted. "I was just talking loudly."

Simon rose and dusted himself off, trying to make his escape.

"I have to make a call," he said, rushing to the door.

"Not so fast," Mrs. Camden replied. "Since you're such busybodies, you, Lucy, and Ruthie will make lunch for everyone. Then we will all sit down together and enjoy it."

She turned to Reverend Camden. "Meanwhile, your father and I will check on the twins."

On the way down the stairs to the kitchen, Lucy was talking a mile a minute.

"There is just no way that Mary is going off to spend half the summer at a beach!" she cried. "Not if I'm stuck here in Glenoak—I mean, Mary can't function without me . . . without us! Not as a lifeguard, not as anything! Someone has to stop her from making a big mistake."

"Who's going to stop her?" Simon asked.

"Dad!" Lucy shot back. "Or Mom. Or Mom should have, but she didn't. Has our mother lost her mind?"

"Susie the Snoop would say we were jumping to conclusions," Ruthie said. "Susie thinks that investigators should get all the facts before they draw conclusions."

"Susie the Snoop is a fictional character," said Simon.

"So is Kermit the Frog. And Hamlet!" Ruthie shot back. "But they both have valid and insightful things to say about the human condition."

Lucy rolled her eyes. "We're not discussing literature here!" she insisted. "We're talking about Mary. This is not one of your silly Susie the Snoop books, Ruthie. This is real life. This is—"

"Mary the Lifeguard," Simon said with a chuckle.

As they entered the kitchen, they spread out. Lucy dug out some pots and pans as Simon raided the refrigerator. Ruthie set the table.

As she filled a pot with water, Lucy shivered.

"Mary the Lifeguard? It's too horrible to contemplate," she cried. "It's crazy."

"Mary's done some stupid things," said Simon as he chopped carrots into a salad bowl. "But I think she's changed. I think she can handle a lifeguard job."

"Oh, really?" said Lucy.

"Yes, really," Simon replied. "In fact, what's bothering you is not that Mary is going to be a lifeguard. What's bothering you is that *you* won't be spending a month at the beach yourself."

Lucy looked up from the pot she was filling. Simon had hit the nail on the head. Lucy was jealous. But she would never let her siblings know.

"So that's what you think?" she said angrily.

"That's what I think," Simon answered. "And I'm sure I'm not alone."

He turned to Ruthie, who had just finished placing the silverware on the table.

"What do you think?"

"I told you what I think," Ruthie replied. "I think what Susie the Snoop thinks. We don't have all the facts, and until we do, I am making no assumptions—about anything. Including Lucy's jealousy or lack thereof."

With that, Ruthie sat down at the table and opened a book. It was the newest Susie the Snoop adventure, fresh from the library.

Lucy pounded the sink. She wanted to scream, so she did.

"There is no way!" she screamed. "No way that Mary is going to spend the rest of the summer—"

"—at Pacific Paradise," Reverend Camden cried, pacing back and forth in the twins' bedroom. "There is just no way Mary is going to spend an unsupervised summer at the beach."

"Quiet, Eric," Mrs. Camden shushed. "Someone will hear you. And Mary is an adult and doesn't need supervision."

"Yes, she does!" Reverend Camden said loudly. "What about that pilot she was dating? He was *my* age, old enough to be her *father*!"

"Quiet," Mrs. Camden insisted. "The kids can hear you." Mrs. Camden covered David and Sam with a blanket. The twins slept like angels in spite of the noise and turmoil all around them.

"What can we do?" Reverend Camden whispered. "I want to give Mary the benefit of the doubt, but I'm not sure she's earned our trust yet."

"She has a job and a place to stay," Mrs. Camden replied.

"Then can't we at least, I don't know, check up on her? Maybe drive up there?"

Mrs. Camden grinned. "Now you're talking!"

"But we'd need an excuse to go to Pacific Paradise and a place to stay," Reverend Camden said, lost in thought.

"Do you remember what Dr. Napier said last month?" Mrs. Camden asked.

Reverend Camden's eyes lit up.

"Dr. Napier's beach house!"

Mrs. Camden nodded. "He said we could use it anytime he and Marjorie aren't. Do you think it will be free this week?"

"I'll call and find out," Reverend Camden replied.

"If the house is empty, we can drive up to Pacific Paradise this weekend and spend a few days," Mrs. Camden said. "I'm sure

Lucy, Simon, and Ruthie would love some time at the beach—"

"To spy on Mary, if nothing else," said Reverend Camden.

"And we could all spend the weekend together," Mrs. Camden continued. "As a family—"

Reverend Camden grinned mischievously.

"One big happy family—of low-down, dirty spies."

TWO

Mary Camden had been driving up the Pacific coast for over two hours. Now she pulled off the main highway and down an exit ramp. By a long, narrow, winding road at the bottom of the ramp, Mary saw a quaint wooden sign surrounded by trees.

PACIFIC PARADISE, 2 MILES

Her heart racing nervously, Mary took a deep breath. Then she turned onto the road and put her foot on the gas.

Robbie's car purred like a dream. The breeze from the open windows stirred Mary's long hair. It was still warm, and the sun was setting through the trees. Mary sniffed. She could already smell the salty tang of the Pacific Ocean.

There was no one else on the road as Mary pulled onto the shoulder. Eager to make a good first impression, Mary brushed her windblown hair and fixed her makeup. When she was satisfied with her appearance, she got back on the road.

Mary couldn't believe her luck. Getting a job at an exclusive resort like Pacific Paradise was a once-in-a-lifetime experience. The place was famous all across the state as one of the great summer resorts, where affluent families took their children for fun in the sun and to get away from the hustle and bustle of the big cities.

A supervisor at Jet Blue who owned a cottage at Pacific Paradise had told Mary about the job and put in a good word for her. Even then, Mary was surprised when someone from the exclusive private resort agreed to talk to her about the job. The interview went well, and Mary was hired three days later.

Mary saw a high iron gate with a guardhouse outside, and nervous butterflies fluttered in her stomach. She slowed to a halt in front of the Pacific Paradise compound, and a sharp-featured man in a security uniform approached the car.

"Can I help you?" the man asked.

"Hi," Mary replied nervously. "I'm Mary . . . Mary Camden. I'm here to see Mr. Broome."

The guard's stony face broke into a wide grin.

"Hi, Mary," he said, now friendly. "I'm Phil Greentree, head of security. Ray's expecting you."

"Great!"

"Just follow this road past the cottages until you see the ocean. On the left you'll find beach headquarters, or 'the beach house,' as the locals call it. It's a big blue building. Ray is waiting for you in his office. I'll call and tell him you're coming."

"Thanks, Mr. Greentree," Mary replied.

"Call me Phil," the man said. Still smiling, he opened the gate and waved Mary on through.

As Mary drove through the streets of Pacific Paradise, she was amazed at how beautiful the exclusive community really was. Neat streets were lined with Spanish-style cottages surrounded by flowers, shrubs, and trees. In the golden light of dusk, the yellow, blue, green, and pink stucco glowed. Luxury cars—BMWs,

Jaguars, and a few Hummers—were parked in front of the beautifully kept houses.

One little yellow house close to the beach caught Mary's eye. It wasn't the trellis covered with blooming roses or the little porch with the wicker chairs that caught her eye. It wasn't even the two birds splashing happily in the birdbath on the front lawn that attracted Mary's attention. It was the name on the mailbox that drew Mary's gaze to the lovely summer place.

"Dr. Richard Napier," Mary said out loud. "I didn't know our family doctor had a house here. I'll have to stop by to say hello sometime."

As she slowly drove along the winding road, Mary saw happy vacationers everywhere. Most were wearing bright summer colors or were wrapped in beach towels. Kids threw Frisbees and played volleyball in a broad grassy park.

As Mary approached the blue stucco house that served as beach headquarters, she could see the white-sand beaches beyond. Gulls wheeled in the bright bronze sky as the setting sun tinted the ocean a bright orange.

When she cut the engine, the sound

of surf and the cries of seagulls filled Mary's ears.

"Are you Mary?" a voice asked.

Mary blinked and looked up. A ruddy, weathered face was smiling down at her. The man opened the car door with a strong, sun-bronzed arm and stepped aside.

"I'm Ray Broome," he said.

Mary climbed out of the car and shook her new boss's hand.

Ray Broome was an older man, about the Colonel's age. He wore a shapeless hat to cover his bald head—no doubt to protect it from sunburn. Mr. Broome had a white glob of sunblock across his wide, wrinkled nose, and his smile was warm and genuine.

"Welcome to Pacific Paradise," he said. "Grab your things and come on into my office."

The interior of the pale blue beach house was surprisingly cool after the heat of the late afternoon. Ray Broome's office was small, with a single worn desk, a computer terminal, a phone, and a big radio.

Ray invited Mary to sit, then pulled out

her file. He paged through some papers, and Mary recognized the forms she filled out to get this job. She tried hard not to fidget in her seat, even though she was very nervous.

"Your credentials are great," Ray said at last. "Even better, you passed your life-saving accreditation with flying colors."

"CPR, too," Mary said with pride.

Ray smiled again. "I think you'll like working here, Mary."

Mary finally relaxed a little. She'd almost forgotten she already had the job. It was nice to hear Ray say it.

"I know you're here late in the season," Ray Broome continued. "I usually like my people to be around for the entire year, but we had one of the veteran lifeguards move on, and I was stuck for a replacement."

"I'll try to fit in," Mary said.

"I know you will," he replied. "At Pacific Paradise we like to treat everyone as family. A big, happy family."

Mary nodded, not sure what to say.

"Most of the folks who come here are professionals from the big cities. They bring their families and want nothing more than peace and quiet. There aren't many young people here—"

Mary's heart sank. Deep down, she was hoping to meet some interesting guys.

"—and no wild parties. Just couples and their kids or grandchildren, here for a good time."

"It sounds nice, Mr. Broome," Mary said.

"Good!" Ray said, rising. "Let's go and meet the folks you'll be working with, then I'll show you the cottage where you'll be staying. I hope you don't mind living by yourself."

"Not at all!" Mary said, relieved she wouldn't be sharing a cottage with a stranger.

Mary grabbed her suitcase. "Leave it," Ray told her. "I'll have Phil Greentree take it to your cottage."

Ray led Mary to a big room lined with lockers.

"This is the ready room," he explained. "The lifeguards assemble here before a shift. Here's your locker. Number 24."

Ray showed Mary how to change the combination. A minute later, two guys came in, laughing and talking. They wore

Speedos and bright orange vests with big letters that read PACIFIC PARADISE LIFEGUARD on the back.

"Bob! Chuck! Meet Mary Camden, the new lifeguard."

The guys came over and introduced themselves. Bob Hopkins was a big blond guy with long hair and a muscular chest. Chuck Telly was shorter, but wide and powerfully built. He had a small tattoo of a bird in flight on his upper left arm. They were both a few years older than Mary.

"And here comes my dumber half," Chuck said, grabbing another guy in a headlock as soon as he entered the room.

"Hi! I'm Dan Telly, Chuck's younger but wiser brother," he said after he escaped his brother's grip. Mary noticed that Dan had the same bird tattoo as his brother—only on his right bicep.

"Where's Sally?" Ray Broome asked.

"Right here, Chief!" a woman said.

Mary turned to see a tall, athletic brunette at least a head taller than everyone else in the room. She wore a two-piece bathing suit like she was born for it. An orange lifeguard vest was casually thrown over her shoulder.

Sally smiled at Mary, then put her arms around Bob and kissed him on the cheek. It was only then that Mary noted they both wore wedding rings.

"I'm Sally," the woman said. "Better known as Mrs. Hopkins."

There was some laughter and kidding around, and soon Mary felt right at home.

"Where are Leigh and Rachel?" Ray Broome asked after a few minutes.

"They were locking up the Surf Shop, last time I saw," Chuck Telly replied.

"Here they are," said Ray. "Mary Camden, meet Leigh Rogers and Rachel Glover. They run the Surf Shop."

Leigh Rogers was blond and petite. She shook Mary's hand and then kissed Chuck Telly. It was obvious they were boyfriend and girlfriend.

Then the girl named Rachel approached. It seemed to Mary that Rachel would rather melt into the walls than meet someone new. Rachel didn't smile, nor would she meet Mary's gaze. Her complexion was pale, and she had long brown hair that drooped over her slumped shoulders.

Mary thought immediately that Rachel

seemed out of place. The other people who worked for Ray Broome were outgoing and athletic, but Rachel was timid and shy. She reminded Mary of a scared rabbit, ready to run at any sign of trouble.

Mary stuck out her hand.

"Nice to meet you, Rachel," she said sincerely. "I hope we'll be friends."

Rachel raised her eyes and met Mary's. She smiled, but her face was still guarded.

"Nice to meet you," Rachel said, barely above a whisper.

Out of the corner of her eye, Mary saw Sally shake her head and walk off toward the changing rooms. Leigh watched her leave and frowned. Sally Hopkins was almost rude, like she wanted to avoid Rachel.

Mary was puzzled. Didn't Ray Broome say everyone at Pacific Paradise was one big happy family?

"Well, let's go, Mary," Ray said before Mary could ask any questions. "I want to show you your cottage."

"Hey, Mary! After you're settled in, come over to the pool hall," Chuck Telly called. "We all get together after work and socialize. Sometimes our mean old skinflint of a boss even shows up."

Ray Broome snorted.

"Thanks for the offer," Mary said. "But I'm pretty tired."

"Do come!" Rachel Glover said. Her voice was insistent, and everyone seemed surprised by her outburst, but Mary smiled warmly.

"Okay, I will!" she said. Then she pointed at Rachel. "And I bet I'll beat you at a game of pool, too!"

Rachel flushed, embarrassed. Then she smiled. "You . . . you're on!"

Outside, darkness had fallen. Brightly colored lanterns lit the way along the narrow streets. Ray pointed to a path that led between some tall trees.

"The employee cottages are through here."

Along a path made of flat, surf-worn rocks stood a line of tiny, rickety cottages. They were constructed of wood weathered white by sun and salt air.

"Here you go," Ray Broome said, stopping before a worn wooden structure that actually leaned to one side. "Number 24—just like your locker."

Ray pushed open the door and snapped on a bare lightbulb. The dusty interior smelled musty and damp.

Mary saw two chairs, a stained table, and a cot. Her suitcase, with bed linens and some beach towels piled on top, sat in the center of the room.

"You'll find the bathrooms and showers at the end of this path," Ray Broome told her. "I know it's not the Ritz, but you'll soon make it feel like home, I'm sure."

With that, Ray Broome wished Mary luck and told her to report to the ready room at eight o'clock in the morning. Sharp!

When Ray was gone, Mary sat down on the cot. It was hard and uncomfortable. Mary lay back, anyway.

She was a little disappointed in her lodgings. Pacific Paradise had such an exclusive reputation, Mary had been hoping to stay in a really nice beach house—maybe one with a view of the ocean. She certainly hadn't expected this cramped, dismal space with one tiny window and a single lightbulb.

Mary sighed, deciding to make the best of things.

Still staring at the ceiling, she decided that even though she was tired, she would change clothes and go down to the pool hall. She'd promised Rachel she'd show up, and she wanted to get to know her new coworkers better.

As she changed her clothes, Mary's mind wandered. She imagined herself in Dr. Napier's marvelous little beach cottage with the happy birds singing as they splashed away in the birdbath.

"Wouldn't that be lovely," she sighed.

THREE

By Mary's third day on the job, things had become pretty routine. Every morning the lifeguards assembled in the ready room, and Ray Broome gave out their assignments. Ray explained that the lifeguards each worked a section of the beach but had walkie-talkies to alert the other lifeguards in case of trouble.

On that first day on the job, Mary had been paired with Chuck Telly, who taught her beach etiquette. She learned when to blow the whistle, when to order someone out of the water, and what to do in case someone started to drown.

"Has anyone actually drowned around here?" Mary asked him.

"Never," Chuck replied. "The people who work here are very responsible. There are no other beaches on either side of us for miles and miles, so the beach is pretty private. We have a limited population in Pacific Paradise, and we control access to all four beaches. The closest beach to Pacific Paradise is up the coast about three miles. A private beach that belongs to the Valley Fountain Lodge, a resort for rich Hollywood types."

"Wow!" said Mary.

"Not that we don't get Hollywood types here, too," Chuck continued. "See that girl in the pink bikini?"

"I noticed her," Mary replied. "And so did every guy on the beach!"

Chuck laughed. "That's Amy Reese. Her parents own the big pink cottage near the park. Amy lives in Los Angeles. She's a model, and she's even been in several television commercials."

Mary studied the girl. Amy Reese stood up and pulled her yellow hair back. With anyone else, it would have been a perfectly innocent gesture. For Amy, it was a cry for attention that worked like a charm—every male on the beach was staring at her.

Even Chuck Telly had a hard time keeping his eyes on the ocean.

"Just looking," Chuck insisted. "I'm really happy with Leigh. We met at the beginning of the season and have been together ever since."

"I've noticed," Mary said, hiding her jealousy. She wondered if she would ever have a relationship like that.

Chuck suddenly blew his whistle.

"Away from the rocks," he said, his voice booming through a bullhorn.

A gang of teenagers moved away from the ragged outcropping of rocks on the far end of Beach 4. Mary had been told that the rules at Pacific Paradise were very strict. Most of the families left their teenagers and younger children to play on the beach unsupervised. It was up to the lifeguards and resort staff to play baby-sitter, and they did it with an iron hand.

"If you can, keep folks away from those rocks," Chuck explained. "There's a nasty riptide over there. It carried a little girl out to sea a few seasons back."

"A what?"

"Riptide," Chuck continued. "It's a vortex of water created by the current and the angle of the rocks. It causes a fast tide that pushes swimmers far out to sea if they're not careful. Like that little girl."

"I thought you said nobody drowned," Mary said.

"I didn't say the girl drowned," Chuck replied. "Only that the riptide carried her off. The girl was ten and floated away on a red air mattress. She floated all night before the Coast Guard found her the next morning. Ray had a fit about that screwup and one of the lifeguards lost his job!"

After that first day, Mary worked on her own. On her second day she sat in the high lifeguard chair, hiding from the glare of the sun under a tiny umbrella she constantly had to adjust to keep in the shade.

Twice she stopped kids from hurting themselves with rough horseplay. Once she banned a little ten-year-old boy named Roger from the ocean for the afternoon because he dunked his little sister and neither parent was around to stop him. At the end of the day, the boy's parents found out what had happened and thanked her.

At night Mary usually hung out with the gang at the pool hall. The little meeting place wasn't for guests, only employees of Pacific Paradise. There were two pool tables, some video games, a soda machine, and lots of free snacks.

A big jukebox played free music until late into the night, and sometimes Ray rented the staff a DVD to watch on the big-screen television.

Chuck and Leigh were tight and Sally and Bob were married, so Mary found herself spending time with Rachel.

Despite their differences, Mary and Rachel got along well. It was just last night that Rachel told Mary about coming to California from her home in Oklahoma.

"My parents died in a car accident when I was twelve," she explained. "Then, during my sophomore year in high school, my only grandmother passed away, too. After that, there was nothing holding me or Paul in Oklahoma, so I dropped out of school and we left."

"Paul?" Mary asked. "Who's Paul?"

"Paul Tilson, my boyfriend," Rachel explained.

Mary was surprised. "I didn't know you had a boyfriend!"

Suddenly Rachel seemed quiet.

Mary persisted. "How come I haven't met your boyfriend yet?" she asked.

"Paul used to be a lifeguard here," Rachel explained. "But he wanted a better position, so he took a job at the Valley Fountain Lodge."

"That fancy Hollywood resort?"

Rachel nodded. "Paul's real busy nowadays, so I don't see him much. I saw him today, but we . . . had a fight."

Rachel pulled her collar tight around her neck. "We patched things up and I'm sure he'll come by this weekend. I'll introduce you to him then."

Rachel continued to fiddle with the collar of her sweatshirt. She was sweating.

"You look uncomfortable," Mary said. "Maybe you should change into something cooler."

"No," Rachel said, pulling her collar tight. "I'm fine. Really. I get cold all the time, so I don't like wearing short-sleeve shirts or shorts or anything like that."

Mary found that odd coming from someone who worked at a surfing store, but she said nothing.

"Come over here, Mary," Bob Hopkins

called, waving a pool cue. "You owe me a rematch."

"Some people like to lose, I guess," Mary replied with a chuckle.

Ray Broome said good night.

"Tomorrow is Friday," he said to Mary on the way out. "Your first weekend here. Things get hectic around here on weekends, so keep on your toes."

"I'm ready!" Mary replied confidently.

"Yeah," Bob butted in. "Ready to lose at pool!"

As they began to play, the other employees gathered around to watch. Mary laughed and had fun, even though Bob beat her this time.

Mary suddenly realized that she felt right at home. Things at Pacific Paradise were settling into a pleasant routine.

Things were anything *but* routine at the Camden household. At the crack of dawn on Friday, Lucy, Simon, and Ruthie were up and packing their things for the drive to Pacific Paradise. Vacations came few and far between for the Camdens, and everyone was excited.

"Have you finished packing yet?" Lucy

asked Ruthie, who was sitting at the kitchen table with a stack of Susie the Snoop books in front of her.

"I finished last night," Ruthie said smugly. "All I have to do is pack my beach reading."

"Where's Dad?" Simon cried as he rushed into the kitchen, suitcase in hand.

"He's in the living room, waiting for Dr. Napier to show up with the key to his beach house," Lucy replied.

Simon grinned. "This is going to be great. Four days of sun, surf, and sand."

"And spying on Mary," Lucy added.

Simon shook his head. "Not me. I'm going to have fun, and I'm going to leave Mary alone."

"Humph!" Lucy snorted. "Some people have forgotten why we're making this trip."

Simon laughed. "Silly me! And I thought it was just a vacation."

Just then, the doorbell rang.

"I'll get it!" Lucy, Simon, and Ruthie called as one. They rushed to the door.

Reverend Camden was already there.

"Dr. Napier!" he said. "Come on in."

"Hello, Reverend," Dr. Napier replied. The elderly man with a full head of gray hair and a gray beard took one look at the Camden kids and chuckled. "I see everyone is ready for their big vacation," he said jovially.

Lucy, Simon, and Ruthie were indeed ready. All three were decked out in beach-wear, including brightly colored shirts, shorts, and beach hats. Ruthie even wore sunglasses that were a tad too large and a swath of sunblock across her tiny nose.

"Here's the key to the cottage, Reverend," Dr. Napier said. "If you need anything, give Phil Greentree a call. He runs a tight ship and can help out with anything."

"I can't tell you how much I appreciate this, Dr. Napier."

"Think nothing of it, Reverend," the physician replied. "After all you did for my son and daughter-in-law, it's the least I could do."

"Oh, Dr. Napier!" Mrs. Camden called from the top of the stairs. "Thank goodness you're here! It will save me a trip to your office. The twins are sick."

FOUR

"I'll have to take some cultures to confirm it, but I'm sure it's strep throat," Dr. Napier declared with a frown. He pulled the stethoscope from around his neck and began to scribble notes on a pad.

"Get this prescription filled, Reverend," the doctor said, handing Reverend Camden the slip of paper. "This medicine will clear up the infection."

The twins were both crying. Their skin was flushed, and they both had a high fever.

Mrs. Camden lifted David and cradled him in her arms. His crying slowed and stopped.

"I came in to wake them up, and they

were both hot," Mrs. Camden explained. "We're lucky you're here, Dr. Napier."

"How did they get exposed to strep throat?" the reverend asked.

"I guess it was their play date the other day with Reverend and Mrs. Chappelle's toddlers," Mrs. Camden replied, not taking her eyes off her suffering boys.

"Oh, no," Reverend Camden cried. "Reverend Chappelle was supposed to fill in for me this Sunday while we were away. But if his kids are sick too—"

Just then the phone rang as if to finish Reverend Camden's thought.

Lucy ran into the room. "Don't answer it!" she cried. She had been listening at the door and suspected that a dreaded phone call was coming.

"Hello," Mrs. Camden said after she lifted the receiver. She spoke for a minute, then handed the phone to her husband.

"It's Reverend Chappelle," she whispered.

Reverend Camden took the phone and spoke for a few minutes. The conversation ended with Reverend Camden saying that he understood and not to worry about Sunday.

"Little Ryan and Roberta Chappelle have both come down with strep throat," Reverend Camden explained. "Needless to say, Reverend Chappelle won't be able to fill in for me this Sunday."

"My, my," Dr. Napier said. "I'd better get on over there and check on the Chappelle children. The twins should be better in a few days as long as they stay put and get plenty of rest."

"There goes our vacation," Lucy moaned. "I'll call Simon and Ruthie up here and give them the bad news."

But Dr. Napier rose and blocked the door.

"You will do no such thing, Lucy Camden," he said sternly.

"Why not?" Lucy demanded.

"The last thing your parents need is five kids with strep throat," the doctor replied.

"Is it likely the other kids will get it?" Reverend Camden asked.

"Not if they're staying at Pacific Paradise," the doctor replied.

"No! Oh, no!" Mrs. Camden cried.

"You can't be serious," said Reverend Camden.

"I am perfectly serious," Dr. Napier explained. "You'll have your hands full with the twins for the next few days. If the other kids stay here, they could pick up the infection. Then you'll have another week of sick kids in the house, and be more run-down and susceptible to getting it yourselves."

"But the kids would be unsupervised," Reverend Camden argued.

"You could go with them, Reverend. You could certainly use the rest."

"That won't work," Mrs. Camden said. "I won't be able to get out of the house for food or medicine if I'm the only one here with the twins."

"And I need to be here to conduct Sunday services," Reverend Camden said.

"I guess Lucy, Simon, and Ruthie will have to go to Pacific Paradise alone," Dr. Napier continued.

"That's crazy! Insane!" Reverend Camden cried.

"Now, now, you're making too much of this," Dr. Napier chided. "There is no way they can get into trouble at Pacific Paradise. It's a private community, with lots of supervision at the beaches and in the park—and you said that Mary is working there."

Reverend Camden nodded. "She's a lifeguard."

"Well, there you are!" Dr. Napier said. "Surely Mary can watch out for the others if that's what you're concerned about."

"Actually, Mary is the one I'm concerned about," Reverend Camden said.

"Mary!" Dr. Napier shook his head. "You have nothing to worry about with Mary. She's got a level head."

"Does she?" Mrs. Camden queried, hugging David close. "Maybe you don't know all the facts, Dr. Napier."

"One thing I do know," Dr. Napier said sternly. "If Simon and Ruthie stay around the house, they will come down with strep throat. Either they get sick, or they go on their vacation as scheduled."

"Wow! This is great!" Lucy was grinning from ear to ear.

"Sorry, Dr. Napier, but this doesn't sound like a very good idea," Reverend Camden said.

Lucy stepped up to her parents.

"Dad. Mom. Think of it this way," she

said. "All we're doing is following doctor's orders! And you know you can trust me. I'm the enforcer, remember? Miss Goody Two-shoes. The girl who does everything right."

Reverend Camden sank down in a chair. "I'm just not sure," he said, rubbing his now-throbbing temples.

"Trust me," Dr. Napier said as he packed up his medical bag. "They'll be fine at Pacific Paradise."

"Okay," Mrs. Camden said at last. "But before anyone leaves this house, we are all going to sit down and set up some strict rules to follow."

"Great!" Lucy said, pecking her mother on the cheek. "Mom, Dad, you won't regret this decision. We'll do everything you want us to; we'll follow all of your rules—I promise."

Reverend Camden nodded and muttered something.

Mrs. Camden frowned, clearly worried.

"I'm going to tell Simon and Ruthie the good news!" cried Lucy. Then she was gone, taking the stairs two at a time.

FIVE

The sun was a gleaming yellow ball in a bright blue sky. The ocean was calm and blue, the white sandy beach smooth and clean. Gulls played in the surf and circled overhead. A warm breeze stirred the leaves in the trees.

Though it was still early, folks were already lining the quaint streets of Pacific Paradise. Beach towels and blankets in hand, they were all heading for the shore.

At beach headquarters, Ray Broome had just finished giving out the Friday morning assignments. Mary gathered up her walkie-talkie, her whistle, some sunblock, a hat, a towel, and the other things she would need on the beach that day.

While the other lifeguards filed out, Mary's supervisor greeted her.

"I hope you're not worried about covering Beach 4," he said.

"Not at all," Mary replied.

"Chuck warned you about the riptide around the rocks, didn't he?"

Mary nodded. "He did, and I'll make sure that no one gets near the rocks, especially children. I don't want a child carried away by the tide on my watch."

"Good," Ray said. "I know I can count on you."

Ray looked around the ready room one last time. "Well," he said, placing his beach hat on his bald head, "I'd better get to work, too."

A few minutes later, Mary was about to leave the ready room when she heard a loud noise. Someone was pounding on a metal locker.

"Come on, come on," a woman's voice pleaded. Mary recognized the voice. It was Rachel's. She sounded frustrated.

Mary investigated and found Rachel Glover standing in front of her locker. She was wearing powder-blue sweatpants and a matching long-sleeve T-shirt.

"I can't believe this," Rachel moaned, brushing a lock of stringy hair away from her face with the back of her hand. "The door is stuck again, and I can't get my stuff."

"Let me help," said Mary.

She grabbed the handle and yanked hard, but the door wouldn't budge.

"It's been like this for weeks," Rachel complained. "I've asked Ray to fix it, but he says the residents come before the employees. He says the handyman is too busy to worry about a stupid stuck locker."

Mary nodded, still pulling on the locker, with both hands now.

Suddenly the door popped open, so abruptly that Mary nearly fell over backward. Stuff spilled out of the locker and onto the floor. Clothes, mostly. Mary helped Rachel gather them up.

"I'm going to take this stuff to my cottage," Rachel said. "No point leaving it in my locker if I can't get to it when I need it."

Mary snatched a pink bikini from the floor. She held it up so it dangled from her index finger.

"You must have a great figure to wear something like this," Mary said.

To her surprise, Rachel snapped the swimsuit out of Mary's hand.

"I—I don't wear that kind of stuff anymore," Rachel stammered nervously.

Mary could see that. Most of the clothes that fell out of Rachel's locker were sweatshirts and baggy pants—the kind of loose, unflattering clothing Rachel always wore.

Seeing Rachel's distress, Mary dropped the subject.

"You know, you can always use my locker if you need one," Mary said after a minute. "I hardly use it at all, and there's plenty of room for your stuff. We can even share, if you like."

Rachel's face lit up with a huge grin. "That would be great. If it's okay with you, that is."

"Of course it's okay with me," Mary replied. "That's why I made the offer."

Together they hauled Rachel's stuff to Mary's locker and packed it in. Mary taught Rachel the combination to the lock and then headed off to work.

"What time is your first break?" Rachel called.

Mary checked her digital watch. "In three hours or so," she replied.

"Come up to the Surf Shop and we'll have lunch together."

"It's a date," Mary called over her shoulder as she took off sprinting to her station on Beach 4.

Mary didn't want to be late. She had responsibilities, and people were depending on her.

"I want everyone to raise their right hand," Reverend Camden said solemnly.

He stood at the head of the kitchen table, gazing sternly down at the others seated there. Lucy, Simon, and Ruthie shifted nervously in their chairs.

Lucy's right hand shot up. Her lips were tight as she forced back a huge grin of excitement. Simon raised his hand next, his eyes staring down at the table in front of him. He knew if he looked up, he'd bust out laughing and ruin everything.

Only Ruthie hesitated.

"I don't think these vows really apply to me," she said. "I don't date, I don't even know why anybody drinks alcohol, and I don't drive a car—let alone too fast."

Ruthie crinkled her nose. "In fact, that part about driving shouldn't apply to Lucy, either. She drives so slowly that the three-hour trip to Pacific Paradise will probably take us twelve hours!"

Lucy stuck out her tongue at Ruthie, who folded her arms and sat smugly back in her chair.

"Ahem," Reverend Camden interrupted. "No one seems to be taking this ceremony in the serious manner in which it is intended. Once again," he said, his voice steady. "Raise your right hand."

Lucy raised her right hand again. Her smile threatened to split her face.

Simon's hand was still extended, so he wiggled his fingers.

Relenting, Ruthie shot up her right hand.

"Repeat after me," Reverend Camden continued. "I—state your name—do solemnly swear that I will not do any of the bad things we have discussed and will do all of the good things we talked about."

Lucy, Simon, and Ruthie swore the oath. They were about to lower their arms when Reverend Camden spoke again.

"We're not done yet," he announced.

"I swear I will call home at least twice a day," he said.

"We swear!" Lucy, Simon, and Ruthie said as one.

"And I swear that I will bring home to my parents a fair and accurate oral or written report about the activities of Mary Camden and not leave out any fact, no matter how much you think it will upset us both or break our hearts."

Simon lowered his hand. "I can't swear to this. Nobody wants to be a snitch."

"I can," Ruthie said seriously. "I'm a natural spy, and these Susie the Snoop books are teaching me new and better techniques."

"I knew I could rely on you, Ruthie," Reverend Camden said. Then he turned to Simon. "Let me put it another way. You have two choices, Simon. You can be a spy for the CIA—that's the Camden Investigation Agency—and spend four glorious days on the beaches of sunny California. Or you can not be a spy and spend a week or two in Buffalo, New York, with the Colonel. I'm sure he'd be delighted to put you to work doing . . . something."

Simon thought about it, then raised his hand.

"I regret that I have but one vacation to give to my family," he said. "Call me double-oh-seven."

"Fine," Reverend Camden said. "Now that it's settled, you can go."

As one, Lucy, Simon, and Ruthie jumped to their feet.

"—Just as soon as we go over some last minute instructions."

Groaning, the kids slumped back into their chairs. Simon banged his forehead on the table and put his hands over his ears.

"Eric!" Mrs. Camden called from upstairs. "David, Sam, and I need your help for a minute."

The cries of the twins almost drowned out Mrs. Camden's plea.

"Wait here, I'll be right back," Reverend Camden said before running up the stairs.

"If we're lucky, we'll get out of here by noon," Lucy whined.

"Noon tomorrow," Simon replied without lifting his head off the table.

Then Lucy's face broke into a wide grin. "But once we're gone—"

Ruthie raised her hand.

"We're on our own!" the girls said together, slapping hands in an enthusiastic high five.

SIX

"Settle down, Roger," Mary ordered, cupping her hands around her mouth to be heard.

The ten-year-old boy let go of his little sister, and she ran ashore. Roger Kelly remained standing knee-deep in the surf. He stuck out his tongue at his retreating sibling, Debbie.

"Go play over there," Mary said, pointing away from the rocks. "And stop dunking your little sister or I'll ban you from the beach again today."

Roger made a face. Mary put her hands on her hips and shook her head.

"I would expect a more mature response from a gentleman," she said sternly.

With that, Roger waded away from the rocks. When Mary turned to check on another pair of swimmers, Roger gazed at her dreamily.

"Roger likes Mary, Roger likes Mary!" Debbie chanted from the shore.

The boy shook his fist at his sister. "Shut up or I'll dunk you again!" he cried.

As Mary scanned the horizon for trouble, she heard someone call her name.

It was Sally Hopkins, looking tall and regal. Mary stared in admiration. Even the silly-looking lifeguard vest looked good on Sally.

"Lunch break," Sally said. "I'm here to watch your beach until you get back."

"I thought Chuck was supposed to take over for me," Mary replied.

Sally laughed. "He was, but Amy Reese is on his beach, so he decided to trade places with me."

"I wonder how Leigh feels about that," said Mary with a shake of her head.

"About what?" Sally asked, scanning the horizon for swimmers.

"About her boyfriend checking out some model on the beach."

Sally shrugged. "They're not married.

Not like Bob and me. It's different for Chuck and Leigh."

"So," Mary said, "how did you and Bob meet?"

"Right here, at Pacific Paradise," Sally replied. "Two seasons ago. We were both lifeguards, and it was the first year for both of us. We got married last year, at the end of the season."

Sally raised her foot to brush sand away. Mary noticed three green-and-gold bracelets circling her ankle.

"Those are nice anklets," Mary commented. "Where can I get one?"

"You'd better go," Sally told her, ignoring the compliment and Mary's question. "I have to be back at my beach in an hour."

"Okay," Mary replied. "I'm just going to grab a quick bite with Rachel. I'll be back on time."

Sally said nothing. But Mary got the feeling that the girl wanted to say something else.

"What is it?" asked Mary.

Sally faced her. "I didn't say anything."

"But you wanted to."

"No . . . Maybe." Sally turned her eyes away from Mary.

"There's something wrong with that girl," Sally said after a pause.

Mary blinked. "Wrong? With Rachel? Like what?"

Still scanning the shoreline, Sally did not reply. Mary felt her temper rising.

"Like maybe she's not pretty or outgoing enough to be one of the in crowd at Pacific Paradise?" Mary said in an angry tone.

Sally looked at her. "I didn't say that. In fact, when she first got here, Rachel was prettier and more outgoing than any of the other girls."

Sally paused again.

"Forget it," she said at last. "It's none of your business or mine. It's Rachel's life. Let her live it. It's not our problem."

"What are you talking about?" Mary demanded. "What's going on?"

"I don't know what's going on," Sally replied, her eyes locked on a gang of swimmers who were making a ruckus. "I don't know if anything is going on. And there's nothing I can do about it, anyway!"

Mary opened her mouth to speak. Just then, Sally raised the whistle dangling from a plastic cord around her neck and blew.

"Okay! All of you! Out of the water, now!" Sally yelled, clapping her hands.

The kids who were making all the fuss marched out of the water. Mary recognized them as a rowdy bunch who knocked over some litter baskets yesterday while skateboarding on the bike path. She was amazed at how the parents of Pacific Paradise seemed to let their children run wild! No wonder the lifeguards were so strict.

Mary watched Sally for a moment, but the girl refused to meet Mary's gaze. So Mary grabbed her gear and headed for the Surf Shop.

Mary found the shop empty of customers. Rachel and Leigh were stacking bottles of sunblock and tanning formula on the shelves.

"Is it lunchtime already?" Rachel asked, flustered.

"Go ahead," said Leigh. "I'll wait until you come back, then I'll have lunch with Chuck."

"Thanks, Leigh," Rachel said gratefully.

Together, Mary and Rachel headed for the Snack Shop. They ordered their food, then sat down at a shaded table to wait.

Rachel had rolled up the sleeves of her

long-sleeve shirt but still seemed to be uncomfortable. Mary wasn't surprised. The air was hot and the sun blazing.

"When am I going to meet that boyfriend of yours?" Mary asked. "I've been here four days and the mystery man hasn't shown up yet."

"Paul is really busy now that he's working at the Valley Fountain Lodge," Rachel explained. "He said maybe he'd come over this weekend, but he hasn't called yet. . . ."

Rachel's sad voice trailed off.

"Do you miss him?" Mary asked.

Rachel shrugged. "I sometimes think he . . . sees other girls. But I'm sure they're just friends. He's friends with Leigh, too, and she has a boyfriend."

"Chuck," said Mary.

Rachel nodded.

"Paul and I knew each other back in Oklahoma," Rachel continued. "We were a couple all through our freshman and sophomore years of high school. When my grandmother died, we both decided to blow off school and come to California together. Paul wanted to be in movies. I didn't care where I lived, as long as I was with Paul."

Rachel reached up and touched her

face. Mary was surprised to see a tear lurking in Rachel's eye.

"After we were here for a while, Paul changed. Now . . ."

Rachel shrugged again and got quiet. Then she said, "Mary, do you mind if I ask you a question?"

"Not at all!"

"Do you think that I'm pretty?"

Mary blinked. "What kind of question is that?"

"It's silly, I know," Rachel said. "But Paul doesn't act like he thinks I'm very pretty or interesting anymore. There are so many really cool, sophisticated girls here in California. How can I measure up?"

"Come on, Rachel," Mary said. "Paul would be crazy to trade you for one of these California bimbos!"

With that, they both laughed.

"I don't know anymore," Rachel said. "He doesn't even want to be around me. I'm sure he's looking at other girls and thinking, 'Why am I stuck with drab old Oklahoma Rachel?' "

Mary patted Rachel's shoulder. "How about we try a makeover, if that's the way you feel?"

"Really?" Rachel asked.

"Really!" Mary replied. "Lucy and I do it all the time when we dump a guy or get dumped. Or when we're just sad or bored, we get a makeover and we feel much better about things."

Rachel was excited now.

"New hair. New makeup. New clothes. New you!" Mary continued. "Nothing makes a girl feel better. Nothing in the world."

"Sounds great!" Rachel cried, her green eyes sparkling.

"Tonight, instead of wasting our time in the pool room watching dumb Jim Carrey movies, let's get ourselves a new look. Together!"

Rachel giggled.

"And the next time Paul Tilson lays eyes on Rachel Glover, he won't even recognize her," Mary added with a mischievous chuckle. "He's not going to see Oklahoma Rachel. He's going to see one of those glamorous California girls every guy seems to drool over!"

"I thought we'd never get out of there," Ruthie said as she buckled her seat belt.

Lucy, sitting behind the steering wheel of the family van, checked the clock on the dashboard.

"Twelve o'clock," she said. "Just as I predicted. Seat belts fastened?"

"Check!" said Simon, giving her a grin and a thumbs-up.

"Affirmative!" Ruthie called from the backseat. "But I think I see the back door of the house opening."

"Start the engine!" Simon yelled.

"We are *so* out of here," Lucy replied, turning the key.

"It's definitely Dad!" Ruthie cried. "And he's waving a piece of paper."

"Oh, no!" Simon cried. "It's another list. Go! Go!"

"I'm going!" Lucy replied, throwing the van into gear and pushing the gas pedal.

"Wait!" Reverend Camden cried. "I forgot to give you this—"

" 'Bye, Dad," Simon called as the van sped away.

"Goodbye," Ruthie said, waving.

"But—"

It was too late. They were gone, and Reverend Camden was standing in a cloud of dust. He looked down at the paper in his hand and shrugged. Then he returned to the house.

"What's going on?" Mrs. Camden said, holding Sam on her lap.

"I forgot to give Lucy this letter from Dr. Napier. The kids were supposed to give it to Mr. Greentree, head of security at Pacific Paradise."

"What's the letter say?" Mrs. Camden asked, dabbing some apple juice from Sam's chin.

"The letter just introduces the Camden family and permits us to have access to Dr. Napier's house."

"Oh, no, Eric!" Mrs. Camden replied. "Does Lucy have the key?"

Reverend Camden nodded.

"It's on the chain with the car keys," he told her. "I guess I'll have to give the security people at Pacific Paradise a call and explain what happened. Otherwise Lucy, Simon, and Ruthie might not be allowed in."

Reverend Camden rose to get the phone.

"They won't be there for at least three hours, so could you fold the clothes in the dryer first?" Mrs. Camden asked. "Then put the wet clothes from the washer into the dryer."

"Okay."

"Then I have a list of things for you to pick up when you go to the pharmacy to get Sam's and David's prescriptions filled."

"Fine, fine," Reverend Camden replied, not sure in which direction to turn, the important phone call he had to make already forgotten.

SEVEN

It was late afternoon, and the sun over Pacific Paradise was just starting to dip toward the horizon. The crowd was thinning out, and there were only a few dozen people left on Beach 4. Most of them were on the sand, playing volleyball, building sand castles, or throwing Frisbees.

As Mary watched over her beach, her walkie-talkie crackled to life.

"Mary Camden, pick up!"

It was Ray Broome's voice.

"I'm right here, Mr. Broome," Mary answered quickly.

"I've sent Sheena Stapleton, a part-time lifeguard, to relieve you," Ray said. "When she arrives, report to Phil Greentree in the parking lot."

"What's going on?" Mary asked nervously.

"Trouble at the front gate," Ray replied cryptically, then hung up.

Five anxious minutes later, a slim girl wearing a Pacific Paradise lifeguard vest came to relieve her.

Mary barely said hello before she snatched up her gear and ran to the parking lot. Phil Greentree was waiting for her in a security van parked at the curb.

Mary climbed into the van. "What's going on?" she asked again.

"We have some people you may be able to identify," Phil explained. "They are being detained at the front gate. They claim to be related to you."

"Oh, no," Mary gasped, red with embarrassment. "It can't be!"

But it was. As they approached the gate, Mary recognized the Camden family van.

"I can't believe my mom and dad would drive all the way to Pacific Paradise just to spy on me," she said angrily.

Phil Greentree snorted. "If they're your

mom and dad, then they've discovered the Fountain of Youth."

Phil screeched to a halt and Mary peered through the shrubbery. She was surprised to see Simon, Lucy, and Ruthie standing next to the van, a Pacific Paradise security guard watching over them warily.

"Do you know these people?" Phil Greentree demanded.

Sheepishly, Mary nodded.

"Hi, Mary," Lucy said with a wave. Ruthie gave her sister a bright smile of greeting. Simon stepped up to Mary.

"Sorry about this," he whispered.

"Is this Dad's idea?" Mary demanded. "Or do I go home and kill Mom?"

"Actually, this was Dr. Napier's idea," Lucy explained.

She told Mary about the vacation, and David and Sam coming down with strep throat, and how Dr. Napier ordered them out of the house.

"And Dad and Mom actually agreed to this?" Mary said incredulously.

"They had no choice," Ruthie chimed in. "Doctor's orders."

"That's great!" Mary snorted.

"Okay," Phil Greentree said as he

emerged from the guard shack. "I called Dr. Napier and he told me what happened. Which one of you is Lucy?"

"That would be me," she replied.

"Follow my security van and I'll lead you to Dr. Napier's cottage. I assume you have the key?"

"Right here," said Lucy.

"You're staying at Dr. Napier's house?" Mary said, aghast.

"Where else would we stay?" said Simon with a shrug. "With you?"

"Arrrgh!" Mary screamed.

"What's the matter?" Ruthie asked.

"Nothing!" Mary turned to Phil Greentree. "Can we go back to the beach now?"

Mary stalked off and climbed into the Pacific Paradise security van. She didn't give her siblings a second look.

Behind the wheel of their own van, Lucy turned to Simon. "Do you think Mary's angry with us?"

"Oh, I don't know," Simon said sarcastically. "Do you?"

"Well, it's not our fault," Lucy said defensively. "We're just following doctor's orders."

"Better let that defense rest," Ruthie

suggested. "From the look she gave me, I don't think Mary's buying it."

"Do you think she suspects we're here to spy on her?" Lucy asked.

"Susie the Snoop says that suspicious people are always suspicious of others," said Ruthie.

Lucy stared at the road ahead of her. "We're toast," she moaned.

Inside the security van, Mary was apologizing to Phil Greentree.

"Don't worry about it," Phil said. "It was just a misunderstanding."

"I'm so embarrassed," Mary continued. "I had no idea they were coming."

"Not to worry," Phil said with a wave of his hand. "In fact, when we get to Dr. Napier's cottage, you can spend a little time with your brother and sisters. Ray already told Sheena that she would be finishing your shift."

Mary smiled.

"I have a better idea," she said. "Since I have the rest of the day off, drop me at the Surf Shop. I have a previous engagement I don't want to miss."

* * *

"Can you believe this place?" Lucy squealed with delight. "It's like a palace. Look, real marble! I hope I can honeymoon in a place like this!"

"This cottage has three whole bedrooms. Three! One for each of us," Ruthie gushed. "I want the one in the front so I can watch the birds take a bath in the morning."

"Even better," Simon cried. "There are *two* bathrooms. One for me and one for both of you." His eyes suddenly looked dreamy. "Imagine, taking a shower whenever you want, without having to wait for one of your sisters to get out of the bathroom."

"You know what?" Lucy declared, setting down her luggage. "I don't care if Mary is angry with us. Staying in a place like this—with a beautiful beach only a block away—is worth it."

"And how," said Simon, and he sank into a plush chair in the sunlit living room.

Ruthie switched on the television. She flipped the channels in amazement.

"Satellite TV!" she declared. "There are over a hundred channels."

Lucy switched the television off. "We're

not here to watch TV. We're here to have fun in the sun and make sure Mary stays out of trouble."

Simon yawned. "Too late for the beach today," he announced, paging through the Pacific Paradise phone book. "But I found the number of a local pizza place—and they deliver."

Lucy sighed contentedly. "In a place like this, even something as dumb as TV and a pizza sounds absolutely delightful."

"Plain?" Simon suggested.

"Pepperoni!" Ruthie cried.

"Veggies!" said Lucy.

"I'll order two pizzas," said Simon as he reached for the phone. "After all, it's our vacation."

Mary found Rachel at the Surf Shop and invited her out to the local mall. Leigh volunteered to close the shop herself, giving Rachel the chance to leave early.

Giggling like teenagers, Mary and Rachel got into the car, cranking the windows down and the radio up. A few minutes later they breezed through the Pacific Paradise security gates and got on the highway.

"The mall is down the road about five miles," Rachel told Mary.

"Do you get out much?" Mary asked. "Away from Pacific Paradise, I mean."

Rachel shook her head. "Not much. I don't think I've gone through those gates all summer."

Mary shook her head. She'd only been working at Pacific Paradise for a few days, and already she was feeling a little claustrophobic. Mary discovered that she was as excited about getting away as Rachel was.

"Wow!" Mary cried as the mall came into view. "This place is huge!"

Rachel nodded. "It has department stores, jewelry outlets, sporting goods, restaurants, and other cool stuff."

"Do they have a beauty parlor?" Mary asked coyly.

"Over there," Rachel said, pointing. "Next to Abrams Department Store."

Two hours later, the girls emerged from Penny's House of Beauty. Rachel's eyes were bright, her face animated as she gazed at her reflection in a store window.

"I can't believe how awesome I look!" she exclaimed.

"Don't underestimate the power of highlights!" Mary declared.

"Or a brand-new haircut," Rachel said. "I never thought I'd cut my hair, but it looks really chic. I love it!"

"Now let's head over there," Mary said, pointing to a cosmetics shop. "You need a killer lipstick to go with your hair."

"Oh, Mary, thanks so much," Rachel gushed.

"My pleasure," Mary replied.

Rachel halted in front of another store and again admired her new look. "I can't wait for Paul to see me now," she cried.

"And I can't wait to meet him," Mary said, smiling, too. "Now hurry up. It's nearly seven o'clock, and we want to hit some more stores before the mall closes."

EIGHT

Ruthie awoke very early on Saturday morning. She opened her eyes to see the golden sunlight of a Pacific morning illuminating her room with a heavenly glow. Wafting through the open window, a salty breeze stirred her hair. She could hear the chatter of birds in the birdbath outside.

Smiling, Ruthie padded barefoot to the window and gazed out. Head resting on her hands, she watched the birds playing in the cool water only a few feet away.

Meanwhile, Simon rose and stumbled through the long hallway to the bathroom. He felt very tired and a little queasy. Too much pizza and TV last night—and into the early morning hours, too.

But after he took a nice hot shower, Simon felt a lot better. He wiped the condensation from the mirror and brushed his teeth. Through a small high window over the bathtub, sunlight poured into the luxurious, marble-tiled room.

When Simon turned off the tap, he could hear the sound of surf pounding in the distance. He smiled. It was going to be a beautiful day!

In Lucy's room, it was another story entirely. Even after the long drive yesterday, Lucy had trouble falling asleep. Maybe it was the excitement of being in a new place. Or maybe she was upset because of Mary's anger at their arrival. Or maybe it was just because she was in a strange bed.

Whatever the reason, Lucy had been awake for much of the night. She knew Simon had gone to bed late, too, because she could hear the blare of the television. He had been watching the sports channel until well after 1 A.M.

Finally Lucy had drifted off into a fitful slumber, only to be awakened by the harsh glare of the morning sun streaming through her bedroom window. The room was hot and stifling, and Lucy threw off her covers. She had gotten chilly the night before and closed the window. Now she felt like she was gasping for air.

Lucy ran to the window and flung it open, taking deep breaths. The sea air seemed to burn her lungs. Suddenly all the things she had been thinking about the night before came rushing back.

This is crazy, Lucy thought. *Why am I taking this stupid oath thing so seriously?*

Yesterday, when she promised her father she would spy on Mary and report on what she was up to, Lucy had thought the whole thing was funny.

But as she lay awake in bed last night, Lucy realized that even though she had treated the whole oath as a joke, she had actually made a promise. Now she was wondering if that had been wise. Or if it was right to spy on her sister.

Pacing back and forth in the pastel-colored bedroom, Lucy wondered what she should do next. In the last year or so, Lucy had begun to realize that even though she was younger than Mary, she felt older and more mature.

Mary was always stubborn, headstrong, reckless, and careless.

Lucy threw herself onto the bed and sighed deeply.

Mary was also bright, bold, courageous, and experimental—traits Lucy admired but didn't possess.

On a good day, Lucy convinced herself that she had other qualities. Lucy told herself that she was smart and cheerful. Responsible. Reliable. And very, very boring.

Lucy almost screamed into her pillow.

Mary was absolutely *never* boring.

Lucy turned over on the bed and rubbed her tired eyes. "As Popeye would say, I am what I am," she said out loud. Lucy forced herself to smile as she climbed out of bed.

I have to be cheerful, and responsible, and reliable, she told herself. *I'm the Camden watchdog, and my goal right now is to keep an eye on Mary—whether she likes it or not.*

If Mary was about to get herself into some sort of trouble, then Lucy decided it was her responsibility to stop her sister before things got out of hand—or to be there to help if they did.

* * *

Mary had just gotten her Saturday assignment from Ray Broome when Rachel showed up. As she rushed across the ready room, Rachel Glover drew stares from the guys. When Dan Telly saw her, he blinked in surprise.

"Who's the new girl?" he asked with a wink.

Even Mary had to look twice to make sure it was Rachel. Her new haircut and the auburn highlights in her chocolate hair looked even better in the morning light, and the new lipstick they'd bought matched the hair perfectly.

Rachel was even wearing a tight new pink top they'd picked out together. Though she was wearing baggy blue jeans, the new shirt, which revealed a daring bit of tummy, made all the difference.

The pink gloss on Rachel's fingernails and toes matched the top perfectly. And her new sandals were really hot.

Rachel Glover had been transformed. Even Sally Hopkins did a double take when she saw Rachel with Mary at their locker.

"I'm so excited!" Rachel exclaimed. "Paul is coming over this afternoon! I haven't seen him in over a week."

"I can finally meet your mysterious boyfriend," Mary said with a chuckle. "And I must say, he's going to flip when he sees you."

Rachel blushed, then twirled in a pirouette.

"You look spectacular, dah-ling!" Mary said, mimicking the accent of the woman they met at the beauty shop the day before.

Both girls giggled.

"Where are you working today?" Rachel asked after she put her stuff in the locker they shared.

"Beach 4—again!" Mary said proudly.

"Wow," Rachel replied, clearly impressed. "That's the most dangerous beach in Pacific Paradise. It's tough to keep people away from those rocks, even with the sign. Kids especially."

"I run a tight ship!" Mary declared, displaying her silver whistle.

"Ray must really trust you!"

"He won't regret it, either."

"I'd better go," Rachel said, glancing at her watch. "I think Paul's arriving at about three o'clock. He wants to talk to Ray Broome about something, then he said he would come over to the Surf Shop."

"See you then!" Mary replied before heading for the beach.

"Excuse me," Lucy said, calling to a stocky young man wearing a lifeguard vest. "I was wondering if you knew which beach Mary Camden is working at today?" Lucy asked, smiling sweetly.

The lifeguard nodded and approached her. Lucy noticed he had a tattoo of a bird in flight on his arm. She also noticed he was *very* cute.

"Sure," the lifeguard replied. "Mary's on Beach 4, about half a mile down this road. It's the very last beach before you get to the cliffs."

"Cliffs?"

"Yeah," he answered. "Beach 4 is the end of the line. Beyond that point it's rocks and cliffs and tidal pools and riptides. Dangerous stuff."

"Wow!" Lucy said, pushing her hair back. "Good thing we have lifeguards around to protect us."

"I'd better go," the lifeguard said. "I have a beach to guard."

"Bye," Lucy said with a wave. "Nice meeting you."

Things are looking up, she thought.

Which was great because the morning had not gone so well.

"I am not going to spy on Mary," Simon had said at the breakfast table. "I don't care about that stupid promise. Dad was wrong to ask us to do this, and it's just wrong to spy. Period."

"But you said you'd do it," Lucy argued. "You promised."

"It was a bad promise," Simon replied. "If I thought Mary was doing something wrong or if she were in trouble, then I would tell Dad and Mom. But she's not. Mary just wants to have a life away from the Camden household, and we can't condemn her for that!"

Lucy knew it was pointless to argue with Simon. His mind was made up. So she tried to recruit Ruthie instead.

"Think of it as a Susie the Snoop adventure," Lucy told her.

"Susie the Snoop only investigates *crimes,*" Ruthie replied. "*The Theft of the Chinese Vase, The Case of the Kidnapped Cat, The Mystery of the Missing Millionaire,*" Ruthie continued, rattling off the titles of her favorite Susie the Snoop mysteries.

"Well, think of it as a mystery," Lucy argued. "*The Mysterious Motives of Mary Camden.* What is she up to? How will she mess up her life again? Can anyone save her?"

Ruthie shook her head. "Cheap melodrama!"

"Don't forget! We made a promise," Lucy said, laying on the guilt.

"That won't work," Ruthie insisted. "Simon is right. Mary has done nothing wrong. No crime, no investigation!"

Lucy knew she'd lost the argument when Ruthie stalked off to her room with some leftover toast to feed to the birds outside her window.

"If no one will help me, then I'm going to do this on my own."

And with that, Lucy put on her bathing suit, got out her beach towel, sunblock, and sunglasses, and went off in search of her sister.

"Beach 4," Lucy said aloud as she straightened her sun cap. Then she started walking, her sandals flapping on the hot paving stones.

NINE

Simon arrived at the beach around eleven o'clock. Before he left the cottage, he had tried to convince Ruthie to come along with him. But Ruthie insisted on, as she put it, "spending the afternoon on the veranda with a good book."

No doubt she was reading yet another Susie the Snoop mystery. Ruthie never seemed to grow tired of them.

Simon walked down to the shore and found a sign that said BEACH 2. A lot of people were there: mostly children, but a few teenagers, too. He walked around, checking things out until the hot, beating sun began to get to him. As he passed a snack shop, Simon decided to buy something to drink.

"Cranberry juice, please," Simon told the guy behind the counter. As soon as he got the bottle, he cracked it and took a big gulp.

"Hey, remember me?" a feminine voice asked. Simon felt the touch of a hand on his arm and turned.

"Excuse me?" Then his eyes got wide.

Standing before him was an attractive teenage girl. She had long blond hair and wore a skimpy white bikini. Her manicured fingernails were painted a deep violet, and she wore a purple anklet on her right leg.

But mostly, Simon's eyes were drawn to hers. The girl had the largest, loveliest violet eyes Simon had ever seen.

"Oh, my mistake!" the girl said, studying Simon's features. "I thought you were a guy I met at Studio City, at an audition for *Everwood.*"

"The television show?" Simon asked.

The girl nodded. "Actually," she said, "you're much cuter than the guy I thought you were."

Simon smiled and hoped he wasn't blushing.

"Amy Reese," the girl said, extending her dainty hand.

"Simon Camden," he replied, taking her hand in his. Her skin felt warm and soft, and Simon felt his heart flutter. He wanted to say something witty, but his coolness factor seemed to have completely disappeared.

"Are you from around here?" Simon asked.

"No way!" Amy said. "I live in Brentwood. I'm only here for a week, getting a tan for my next modeling shoot."

"Wow," Simon said. "You're a model?"

Amy Reese tilted her head. "And you're not? I'm surprised. In Los Angeles a guy as cute as you are could get plenty of work. Modeling. Work as an extra on television and in the movies. Maybe even a speaking part. Shows with teenagers are hot now, and producers are always looking for new talent."

"You don't say!" said Simon. "Maybe I can buy you something to drink, and you can tell me all about it."

Amy's pretty face burst into a huge grin. "I thought you'd never ask."

By one o'clock, Mary was sick and tired of Lucy spying on her.

At eleven, Lucy had found her sister and claimed a spot close to her lifeguard chair. Lucy spread out her blanket, rubbed some sunblock on her shoulders, lay back on the blanket, opened a magazine, and pretended to sunbathe.

She's not fooling me! Mary thought angrily. *There are two and a half miles of beach here at Pacific Paradise. Why did she camp right next to me?*

Of course, Mary knew the answer. Lucy was a spy.

Mary fumed. She was so angry, it was hard not to let her feelings get in the way of doing a good job.

Pretending that Lucy wasn't there helped a little. Some rough horseplay by a bunch of teenagers playing water football also helped to distract her.

Mary jumped down from her post. The sound of her whistle cut the air.

"Take your game elsewhere," Mary commanded. "Away from the little kids—before you hurt someone."

"Sorry," one of the guys called back as the gang moved off.

Mary spotted Roger Kelly and his little sister, Debbie. They were swim buddies again. She suddenly felt sympathy for ten-year-old Roger. *The poor kid. He probably hates having to drag his little sister around with him everywhere he goes,* she thought.

Mary fought the urge to peek in Lucy's direction. *I sure know how Roger feels. Right now, dunking your little sister sounds like a perfectly reasonable idea.*

Mary scanned the beach. Roger and Debbie's parents were nowhere in sight. As usual. But at least the kids weren't in the water. Today Roger seemed content to help Debbie build a sand castle.

Mary decided to keep an eye on the two of them. Kids on the beach without parental supervision were accidents waiting to happen.

Soon Mary's attention was drawn to a lone swimmer in the distance. She blew her whistle and called to him. Then she used the bullhorn.

"You! In the red swimsuit. Where's your swim buddy?"

Someone at least fifty feet away waved at Mary.

"Stick together, boys!" Mary warned them. "The surf is a little rough today."

And so it went for the next couple of hours. Before long, Mary didn't have to pretend Lucy wasn't behind her, watching her every move. Mary was so busy being a lifeguard, she simply forgot.

The hours passed. Finally, Lucy checked her watch. She was fuming now.

How much longer is Mary going to continue this charade? Lucy thought. *She's ignored me for the last two hours. Never even looked in my direction once.*

From behind her sunglasses, Lucy's eyes followed her sister as Mary applied first aid to a woman who had twisted her ankle in the sand.

Who does Mary think she is? Lucy wondered. *A character out of* Baywatch? *Well, if she can play this game, then so can I.* Lucy flopped on her tummy and tried to apply some lotion to her back.

"Can I help?" a voice asked. Lucy looked up to see the lifeguard who'd directed her to Beach 4 earlier. He was wearing sunglasses now, but she recognized the bird tattooed on his arm.

"Thanks," Lucy said shyly.

"Don't worry, I won't bite," the lifeguard said. Then he pointed to the tube of sunblock. "May I?"

Lucy nodded, and the lifeguard rubbed some lotion on her shoulders. "Thanks . . . I don't know your name."

"Dan," he said. "Dan Telly."

"I'm Lucy Camden. Pleased to meet you, Dan. Again."

"Camden?" Dan said. "Any relation to Mary Camden?"

"She's my sister."

"I should have known that," Dan replied, snapping his fingers. "Anyone as cool as Mary would naturally have a cool sister."

Dan stood up and dusted his hands.

"Well, duty calls," he said. "Maybe we'll meet again."

"I really think you'd be great, Simon," Amy Reese said sincerely. "You're such a hottie."

Simon smiled at the compliment. Amy Reese was full of compliments. She told him she liked his hair, his chin, and his "soulful gaze."

"And I really dig your earring!"

"Thanks. How long have you been

working in Hollywood?" Simon asked.

"Since I was a baby," Amy explained. "When I was seven months old, my picture appeared on a cereal box—Biggie Baby Bran. That gig really kick-started my career."

"And you think I can get work like that? Modeling, I mean."

Amy leaned close to Simon, as if she were going to whisper a secret. He bent down, and her soft lips brushed his neck.

"I think you're made for Hollywood, Simon Camden," she purred.

"There you are!" said Ruthie.

Simon whirled around to see his little sister standing behind him. She had a droopy yellow-flowered sun hat on her head and a Susie the Snoop book under her arm.

"I thought you were going to stay back at the cottage and read," Simon said.

"I was," Ruthie explained. "But the birds were making so much of a racket, I had to escape. So I came out to find you."

"Why don't you find Lucy instead?" Simon asked as he shot Ruthie a "get lost" look.

Ruthie just smiled. "Somehow I think

all the action is around here. With you and Pamela Anderson here."

"Who is this little . . . creature?" Amy Reese asked, barely hiding a sneer.

"My sister," Simon replied.

"How . . . charming," Amy said evenly.

"Don't you have somewhere to be?" Simon said.

But Ruthie just shook her head.

"Look!" Simon said sharply. "Go find Lucy. Or Mary. Or go read your book. You said Susie the Snoop books were the perfect beach reading. Right?"

Ruthie nodded.

"Well, here's a beach. You've got the book. So read!"

Ruthie blinked in surprise.

"Okay! Okay! You've made your point," she said as she walked away. "I'll go find Lucy."

"Are all of your sisters that delightful?" Amy Reese asked when Ruthie was gone.

"Pretty much," Simon said.

Amy smiled and put her arms around Simon's neck.

"Now what were we about to do before we were so rudely interrupted?" she asked, just before her lips touched his.

* * *

"I don't think we're supposed to be out here," Debbie said, her voice quaking. The little girl stumbled and nearly fell into a crab-filled tidal pool of bubbling water nestled between two huge rocks.

"Don't be a wimp," Roger said. "You wanted some rocks for the castle. You said we needed a door."

"I changed my mind," Debbie replied. "And the sign says we're not supposed to be out here, anyway. I can read it, too, you know!"

"Wow! Look what I found," Roger cried, holding up the tattered remains of a dead crab.

"Yuck!" Debbie squealed. "Put it down."

"It will look great on the castle," Roger said. "Trust me."

"This is dumb. I'm going back," Debbie said, turning around. She took a few steps and found herself standing on the edge of a big rock, the ocean waves pounding at her feet.

"Wait!" Roger cried.

Debbie stopped and turned to her brother.

"Take this with you!" Roger cried. He

threw the dead crab to his sister.

As the gruesome thing flew at her, Debbie jumped backward and lost her balance. Screaming, the little girl plunged into the crashing ocean waves!

TEN

Mary caught sight of the splash out of the corner of her eye. She heard the little girl scream a split second later. The girl had plunged into the water perilously close to the rocks. The dangerous tide that swirled past them could carry a child out to sea or drag her down in a minute.

Mary snatched up her walkie-talkie.

"Mayday! Mayday!" she cried, following the procedure Chuck Telly had taught her.

"Beach 4, Beach 4. Swimmer in the water!"

Then Mary took off at a dead run toward the rocks.

As she ran, Mary blew her whistle.

"Everybody out of the water!" she cried.

On the beach, people were now alerted to trouble. All eyes—including Lucy's—followed Mary Camden as she raced across the beach.

Mary jumped and landed on the jagged boulders. She stifled a yelp of pain but kept going as the sharp rocks bruised her feet.

Halfway across the rocky outcropping, Mary found Roger Kelly. The boy was pale and shaking with fear. Tears were streaming down his face.

"Off the rocks!" Mary cried.

"But my sister—"

"Now!"

As Mary raced past the boy, her eyes never left the stricken girl in the water.

Debbie was kicking and screaming. Mary suspected the girl knew how to swim, but the tide was too strong for her to struggle against it for long.

From somewhere behind her, Mary heard whistles blowing and bullhorns booming. The other lifeguards had arrived and were clearing the water. Everyone on the beach was standing now, straining to get a look at the life-or-death drama unfolding before their eyes.

In the crowd, Lucy watched apprehensively. She feared for the safety of the little girl and her sister, too.

On the rocks, Mary was reaching the end of the outcropping. The tide was moving swiftly, dragging Debbie farther and farther out to sea.

"I'm coming," Mary called. "Don't panic!"

But the girl was nearly finished. Debbie's kicks were growing weaker, and her screams had turned to racking sobs and gasps for air.

Mary knew it was now or never.

Extending her arms above her head, Mary put her hands together. She gazed at the rocks below and judged how far she would have to leap to avoid them.

Then she dived.

Mary struck the pounding surf with barely a splash and kicked away from the rocks. The tide grabbed her immediately and tugged her along. The tide was formed when the natural current streamed past the outcropping of rock, narrowing the normally gentle tide into an invisible conveyor belt that lurked just under the surface of the ocean, waiting for a victim.

When Mary's head burst out of the water, she gulped air. Then she spotted Debbie in the churning water about twenty feet away. The girl was hardly struggling at all now.

Mary turned over and did a quick backstroke. In the crashing waves, it was easy for a swimmer to get confused and swim away from land. Once Mary grabbed the girl, she wanted to swim toward the beach, not away from it. Swimming on her back, Mary could clearly see the beach.

She also spotted some of the lifeguards climbing over the rocks toward her. Bob Hopkins was in the lead. His wife, Sally, was carrying Roger Kelly off the rocks and onto the sand.

Now that she was oriented, Mary flipped over again and started to swim as fast as she could toward the little girl. It seemed to take forever to reach her, but Mary knew it probably wasn't more than half a minute. She could feel the pull of the tide and used it to increase her speed.

But in the back of her mind, Mary knew she would have to fight against that tide to get back to shore. And she would be dragging little Debbie with her, too.

Mary's heart skipped a beat. For a split second, she wondered if she would be able to make it. Mary was afraid she would be pulled down by the riptide, along with the helpless child. Then she pushed all such thoughts aside to concentrate on the task at hand.

Mary ducked underwater and kicked her legs in powerful strokes. When her head broke the surface, Debbie was floating right in front of her. The girl's face was pale, but she was still kicking, still alive.

"Got you!" Mary gasped, snatching Debbie's arm.

Mary's lifeguard training had taught her that this was the most dangerous moment in a water rescue. Sometimes victims were so filled with panic, they would lash out at their rescuer. There was even a danger that both could drown. That danger was multiplied by the racing tide that carried them along.

Luckily, as soon as Mary touched Debbie's arm, the girl grew still and allowed Mary to gather her close.

"Can you float?" Mary said, her own lungs burning for air.

The pale face in front of her nodded.

Debbie's lips were tinted blue, and she was shivering. Only then did Mary notice how cold it was in the deep water. Her muscles ached, but Mary knew it was time to start swimming toward the shore.

Mary placed the girl under her arm and began to kick. Despite the tide that pushed at her, Mary inched toward the shore. Each kick, each stroke was a titanic effort as the water dragged at her legs. The rocks loomed ahead of her, but so far away. The beach itself was invisible—the towering waves blocked it from view.

The panic she felt earlier gripped Mary again, and again she shook it off. She knew she could drown, but worrying about it only put her and the helpless little girl under her arm in more danger.

Mary knew she had to focus on the next stroke, the next kick, and trust that God would do the rest.

Mary was glad she had gotten her bearings earlier. Knowing which way to go helped to dull the fear a little. Ignoring her burning lungs, her aching muscles, Mary swam as hard as she could—as hard as she ever swam before.

"Hang on, Debbie," Mary gasped, her

voice choked. She spit out ocean water and kept on swimming.

Seconds later, Mary heard the sound of an outboard motor. A Coast Guard boat, Ray Broome standing on its bow, was racing across the water toward her. Mary waved at the boat. The moment she stopped treading water, the tide caught at her legs and pulled her backward.

When the boat was only a few feet away, the engine was cut and momentum carried it closer to Mary. A lifesaver splashed in the water right near her head. When Mary grabbed it, she felt a rush of relief.

I'm alive!

Strong hands pulled the little girl from Mary's weakened grip.

Then someone jumped into the water next to her. Powerful arms grabbed Mary and lifted her onto the boat. She flopped to the bottom, gasping like a fish out of water.

"Take slow, deep breaths," a Coast Guard sailor told her. Then he put an oxygen mask over Mary's face.

Mary watched the other sailors crowd around Debbie Kelly. For what seemed like an eternity, the girl didn't move.

Then Mary heard Debbie cough, then start to cry. The sailors cheered and slapped one another on the back. Someone put an oxygen mask over Debbie's mouth and a blanket over her shoulders.

Mary shivered, and someone draped a blanket over her shoulders, too. Ray Broome appeared in front of her.

"Is Debbie okay?" Mary asked, her voice distorted by the plastic mask.

Ray Broome nodded. "Thanks to you," he said as he drew the blanket tightly around her shoulders.

Everyone on the beach watched apprehensively as the Coast Guard rescue boat approached Beach 4. Though everyone saw the rescue, no one knew if the little girl was okay or not.

Then the crowd saw Mary stand, a blanket wrapped around her shoulders. Next to her, little Debbie stood up on wobbly knees. Mary reached out to steady the girl. As the flat bottom of the Coast Guard boat scraped the sand, the crowd broke into wild cheers and applause.

Just then, Mr. and Mrs. Kelly arrived, racing through the surf to lift their daughter out of the boat. Mrs. Kelly, sobbing, cradled her little girl in her arms.

With Ray Broome's help, Mary stepped out of the boat. Her knees felt weak, her legs wobbly. She blinked and pushed back the strands of limp wet hair that covered half her face. Only then did Mary notice the applause and cheers.

"Thank you so much!" Mr. Kelly said, shaking Mary's hand gratefully. "You're a real hero."

Others were congratulating Mary, too. Including Bob Hopkins, Dan and Chuck Telly, and a horde of people Mary didn't even know. Even the normally imperious Sally Hopkins seemed impressed.

Ray Broome wrapped his arm protectively around Mary's shoulders.

"Come on, everyone," he said. "Give the girl some room to breathe."

Mary stumbled across the sand, still unsteady. People began to back away, but all complimented her. Some reached out and slapped her on the back.

Suddenly Lucy appeared in front of her. Ruthie was there, too, wearing an incredibly silly yellow hat.

For a moment their eyes met. Then

Lucy reached out and hugged her sister.

"I am so proud of you," Lucy said.

All her anger and pettiness forgotten, Mary hugged back. She clung to her sister as tears of gratitude rolled down her cheeks. Mary was glad to be alive and glad to see a member of her family again.

She didn't know what she would have done if Lucy and Ruthie hadn't been there. She almost died today, and she knew it.

Mary began to cry, and so did Lucy. Even Ruthie, who clung to them both, was starting to get misty-eyed.

"I love you," Mary whispered. "I love you both!"

"And we love you, Mary," Lucy replied.

Once again, the people around them started to applaud. Mary hugged Lucy tighter.

Fifteen minutes later, Mary, Lucy, and Ruthie walked arm in arm toward the big blue beach house. Ray ordered Mary to report to the staff doctor for a quick examination.

They had left the other lifeguards behind to restore order on the beach. Soon people were back in the ocean, having fun again. By the time the Camdens reached the beach house, everything seemed perfectly normal again.

Just another sunny Saturday afternoon at Pacific Paradise.

Suddenly Simon appeared, hand in hand with the lovely Amy.

"What did I miss?" he asked.

"Oh, nothing," Ruthie replied. "Just Mary saving the life of a drowning girl, that's all."

Simon blinked. "You're kidding!"

"No, she's not," said Lucy, squeezing Mary's hand. "Our sister is a hero!"

"I am not," Mary insisted.

"Your boss said you were," said Lucy. "I heard him. And that's good enough for me!"

"Simon, introduce us!" Amy Reese insisted.

"Oh! I'm sorry," Simon said. "This is my sister Mary. She's a lifeguard here. And my other sister, Lucy . . . You already met Ruthie. This is Amy Reese," Simon continued. "She's from LA."

"Pleased to meet you," Amy said.

Ruthie folded her arms and tapped her foot in the sand. "Shouldn't we be moving along? Mary is supposed to see the doctor."

"Doctor!" Simon cried. "Are you hurt?"

Mary waved her hand. "It's nothing," she said. "Just a precaution."

"Go!" Simon said, stepping aside. "See the doctor. We'll talk later."

As Mary, Lucy, and Ruthie walked away, Simon watched them go.

"Your sister Mary is really something," Amy Reese said. "She must take after you."

"Actually, I take after her," Simon replied. "She's older than me."

"Whatever," Amy said, squeezing his hand. "Let's go somewhere private and . . . talk."

As Mary came out of the doctor's office, Rachel Glover was in the waiting room with Lucy and Ruthie.

"Oh, Mary," Rachel cried. "Are you okay?"

Mary smiled for the first time since the rescue. "I'm fine. I feel great!"

Lucy smiled then, too. "What a relief," she said.

"Have you met Rachel?" Mary asked.

"We've met," Lucy replied with a smile. "You have a nice friend."

"Yes," Ruthie said. "Rachel was telling me about her secret place. Where she goes to be alone and think." Then Ruthie looked up at Rachel. "But she didn't tell me where her secret place was."

"If I did that, it wouldn't be a secret," Rachel replied. Then she turned to Mary. "You're a hero, Mary!" Rachel exclaimed.

Mary blushed.

"Ray came up to the shop and told everybody about it. He's going to throw a rescue party tonight in your honor!"

"A what?"

Rachel laughed. "A rescue party. It's kind of a traditional celebration around here. If someone gets rescued, then Ray throws a party in honor of the lifeguard who did the rescuing."

"I—I don't know what to say," Mary stammered.

"Don't say anything," Rachel replied. "Just have fun. And bring Lucy and Ruthie and whoever else you want to bring! Everyone's invited."

"Will your mysterious boyfriend be there?" Mary asked.

Rachel's eyes went wide. "Oh, no!" she cried. "In all the excitement I forgot. Paul is probably at the Surf Shop now, waiting for me."

"Well, let's go," Mary said. "I want to meet him."

Out of the corner of her eye, Lucy caught sight of Dan Telly.

"I'll see you later," Lucy said, excusing herself. "I have something I've got to do."

"I'm going with Mary and Rachel," Ruthie said excitedly. "For some reason, I think the fun is just beginning!"

ELEVEN

On their way to the Surf Shop, Mary, Rachel, and Ruthie stopped off at the ready room.

Mary opened up her locker and found some dry clothes. Then she changed out of her damp bathing suit. Rachel reapplied some makeup, using the mirror inside the door of the locker they both shared.

"I want to look absolutely stunning when I see Paul," Rachel explained.

While Ruthie played with her lifeguard vest, Mary dried her long hair with a towel and brushed it. Rachel was in such a hurry that they left after that. Mary's hair was still damp as they walked together to the store.

As they entered the Surf Shop, Mary saw a hard-faced blond guy standing with Leigh. He seemed to have a permanent scowl affixed to his face. His jaw was lined with stubble, like he hadn't shaved in a few days. He wore a black heavy metal T-shirt and baggy shorts.

The guy turned and spotted the three of them. He didn't smile. He just shook his head as Rachel rushed forward to hug him.

"Oh, Paul," she gushed. "It's great to see you."

Then Rachel stepped back, waiting for Paul Tilson to compliment her on her sexy new look. Instead, he turned and faced Mary.

"Who's this?" he demanded.

"That's my new friend, Mary," Rachel said quickly. "Mary Camden. And that's her little sister Ruthie. Mary just rescued a little girl on Beach 4."

"Yeah," Paul snorted. "I heard. Ray Broome was in here gassing on about the whole thing a few minutes ago—before he blew me off."

"That rescue was really something, Mary," Leigh chimed in.

"Does that mean Ray is going to throw

one of his stupid rescue parties tonight?" Paul Tilson asked, still scowling.

"Yes," Rachel said, her voice softer now. "You can come . . . if you want to."

She lowered her eyes, refusing to meet his.

Mary thought that Rachel had been coming out of her shell, but as soon as she was with Paul, she seemed to crawl right back into it again.

"Don't you want to come?" Rachel asked meekly.

"Sure," he said with a smirk. "I wouldn't miss it for anything." As he spoke, Paul never took his eyes off Mary.

Mary felt uncomfortable under Tilson's gaze. He seemed hostile, and Mary didn't like him from the moment they met.

"Mary!" Ray Broome called from the door. "I was looking for you."

Mary smiled, relieved by any interruption that took her away from Paul Tilson.

"The Coast Guard wants you to file a report," Ray told her. He held open the door, motioning Mary forward. "It's just a formality. Everybody around here thinks you're a real hero," Ray said with a note of pride.

Mary blushed. *I wish everyone would stop calling me a hero,* she thought. Even though it felt pretty good!

"You heard about the party tonight?" Ray continued, stepping into the shop. "It's in your honor, you know."

"Really, Mr. Broome," Mary said. "You don't have to do this."

"Nonsense!" Ray replied. "It's a tradition around here. You don't want to buck tradition, do you?"

"No," Mary said. "Of course not."

"Great!" Ray said. "Now come on over to my office. Coast Guard captain Fred Fletcher is waiting to talk with you."

"Sorry, Ruthie," Mary said. "Duty calls."

"That's all right," Ruthie replied. "I have my book to read."

Before Ray Broome left, he turned to Paul Tilson.

"Sorry I had to miss our appointment," he said. "We had a lot of excitement around here this afternoon."

"Sure," Paul said, frowning.

"Come by my office tomorrow morning, and we'll meet then."

With that, Ray Broome led Mary out of the Surf Shop.

"I'm going out for my lunch break," Leigh told Rachel. "I'll be back here in an hour or so."

After they left, Ruthie hung around the Surf Shop. She wanted to get to know Rachel, and they talked for a little bit. But things got busy in the store and Rachel, who was alone in the shop, had to take care of the customers.

Ruthie wandered the aisles, checking out all the stuff for sale. She found a rack of postcards and looked through them for what seemed like a long time.

The store was finally empty again, so Ruthie went off to search for Rachel. She found her in the T-shirt section with her boyfriend, Paul. They were talking intently and walking in Ruthie's direction.

Ruthie made a snap decision and melted into the clothing racks. She was invisible to Paul and Rachel, and they approached her.

"Mary isn't like that," Rachel said, her voice tense. "She's really nice."

"Nice!" Paul grabbed Rachel's arm and squeezed it.

"You're hurting me, Paul," Rachel squealed.

"You always say that," Paul shot back. "It's just another plea for sympathy. That's what you want. Pity."

"Let go!" Rachel cried.

Ruthie's eyes got wide. Her heart raced. She was frightened and didn't know what to do, so she just buried herself farther into the clothes.

Paul Tilson tightened his grip. His powerful fingers were digging into Rachel's arm.

"Poor me, my grandma died!" Paul taunted her. "Poor me, my folks got killed in a car crash! Poor me, my boyfriend works around a bunch of pretty rich girls and I'm so jealous, I can't take it!"

"I never said that," Rachel cried, trying to pry his fingers loose with her other hand.

"You hate it that I want something more than a dump like Pacific Paradise," Paul said. He was shouting at Rachel now. "You're afraid I'll dump you for a pretty girl," he continued, shaking her. "And that's what I ought to do!"

"Please," Rachel gasped, a tear staining her cheek.

"Why else would you dress like that!"

Paul shouted. "Well, forget it! You're not pretty enough to wear those kinds of clothes. You just look dumpy and stupid!"

With that, Paul ripped the sleeve of Rachel's brand-new top. "Go back to your cottage, you dumb Okie girl," Paul shouted. "Go put some clothes on. Cover yourself up."

He pushed Rachel into a rack of clothes. Ruthie couldn't see either of them now. But she could still hear Rachel's cries.

Then Ruthie heard a smack, and Rachel howled. Then another smack. Now Rachel was sobbing.

Ruthie heard a scuffle, and Rachel stumbled into view again. Paul stormed in right behind her, crowding her.

Paul shook his fist in Rachel's face and she drew back fearfully, covering her face with her hands.

"You're not worth it," Paul said, lowering his fist again. He gave Rachel one last push, then stormed out of the store.

Rachel stood among the racks of T-shirts, fingering her ripped shirt and crying. Her hair was disheveled, her makeup running as it mixed with her tears. Then

Rachel ran into the stockroom and slammed the door behind her.

When the coast was clear, Ruthie stuck her head out from among the shirts. She scanned the room, fearful that Paul Tilson was still lurking somewhere nearby.

When Ruthie was convinced it was safe, she ran out of the store as fast as she could.

As the sun began to set, Lucy and Simon met back at the cottage.

"You didn't waste any time finding a new friend," Lucy said coyly.

Simon grinned from ear to ear. "Neither did you," he replied. "I saw you and that lifeguard talking together. He was having trouble concentrating on his work with you around. I wonder what Kevin would say about that?"

But Lucy just grinned.

"Our relationship is friendly, and that's all. His name is Dan Telly. He and his brother are both lifeguards here. Dan is thinking about going to divinity school. I was telling him about my divinity classes."

"Cool," Simon said with a nod. Then he asked about Ruthie.

"She's still with Mary, I guess," Lucy replied. "I took off to talk with Dan and just lost track of time. He's going to be my escort to the rescue party."

"The what?"

"Rescue party," Lucy explained. "It's tonight. At beach headquarters. The party is in Mary's honor, seeing as how she's a hero and all. Everybody's invited."

"Great!" said Simon. "I'll bring Amy." Then he checked his watch. "I'd better call Amy and get ready."

"I better get ready, too!" Lucy cried, rushing to her bedroom.

Ruthie ran, but not too far. She slowed down when she realized nobody was following her. Then she began to wonder if Rachel was okay.

Ruthie thought about finding Mary and telling her all about what happened but decided she would try to talk to Rachel first.

Cautiously, Ruthie returned to the Surf Shop. There was no sign of Rachel anywhere. Only Leigh was working busily behind the counter.

Remembering that Rachel and Mary

shared the same locker, Ruthie hurried over to the ready room. There were people all over the place, and Ruthie had a hard time trying to sneak inside.

It turned out she didn't have to. Rachel came out of the beach house a few minutes later. She was wearing baggy sweatpants and a hooded sweatshirt, and Ruthie hardly recognized her. A beach towel was slung over Rachel's shoulder.

Ruthie thought about calling out to Rachel but decided to follow her instead. The words of Susie the Snoop rang in her ears. "People won't always tell you the truth," said Susie. "But they will show you the truth sometimes if you just keep quiet and follow them."

So that's what Ruthie did.

Rachel walked and walked. She passed Beach 1, 2, and 3 without a second glance.

All the while, Ruthie followed. Not close enough to be seen but not far enough away to lose Rachel.

Just like Susie the Snoop would do.

When they arrived at Beach 4, Ruthie was convinced Rachel would settle down. But to her surprise, Rachel Glover kept on walking, to the end of the beach and past the rocks where Mary had leaped to that little girl's rescue only a few hours before.

Ruthie watched as Rachel hopped the low fence. Ignoring the warning sign, Rachel kept on going. Ruthie paused, waiting until no one was looking. Then she jumped over the fence, too, and followed Rachel.

They walked for a long time, Rachel in the lead, Ruthie trailing behind her. The shoreline got rugged and more savage. There was no beach here. No white sand. No lifeguards. Only a cliff made of jagged rocks that rose higher and higher.

It was wild and dangerous, but Rachel seemed to know the way. She hopped from rock to rock, high over the crashing waves.

Ruthie had a hard time keeping up—her legs weren't as long as Rachel's.

Finally, Rachel paused. She turned to scan the area, and Ruthie had to duck behind a rock to avoid being seen. When Rachel thought the coast was clear, she scampered down a path between some rocks and vanished from sight.

Ruthie cautiously crept forward and looked down. She could see Rachel far below. The girl was sitting on a flat boulder in front of a rocky cave. Twenty feet below the ledge, the waves crashed between the rocks with a deafening sound.

The sun was starting to set now. The rocks around Ruthie cast long shadows in the fading sunlight. The roar of the surf in this wild place was scary, and Ruthie wanted to go home.

But first she had to discover just what was really going on.

Patiently, Ruthie watched as Rachel spread out her beach towel. Then the girl unzipped her hooded sweatshirt and peeled it off, along with her sweatpants.

When Rachel tossed her clothes aside, Ruthie gasped.

Rachel wore nothing but a pink bikini, and the skimpy swimsuit could not hide the purpling bruises on her arm and on her shoulder, where Paul had grabbed her that afternoon. There were also more faded-looking bruises all over the girl's back and legs.

Ruthie was convinced that she'd found Rachel Glover's secret place and discovered the girl's terrible secret, too.

Rachel's boyfriend, Paul Tilson, was abusive. The violent episode she'd witnessed and the resulting bruises were all the proof that Ruthie needed.

Ruthie turned around immediately and headed back to Pacific Paradise. As she climbed over the rocks, her mind raced at top speed.

Ruthie wasn't sure what she should do next. But she knew she had to do something, before Rachel Glover ended up with far worse than a few ugly bruises.

TWELVE

Ray Broome's traditional "rescue party" was in full swing when Mary arrived. Colorful party lights were strung up all over the ready room. A table sitting in a corner groaned under the weight of snacks and drinks.

To greet the guest of honor, someone had hung a huge hand-painted banner with big red letters that read:

MARY CAMDEN: HERO OF THE HOUR

The music stopped, and everyone jumped to their feet and applauded as Mary entered the room.

"This has got to stop!" Mary said, laughing. "But I have to say a girl could get used to all this attention."

The crowd roared with laughter. Someone handed Mary a soda, and the music started up again. Everyone was dancing and having fun.

Mary came to the party wearing a pale blue sundress and sandals. Her outfit drew stares from many of the guys.

Mary ignored them for the time being. Instead, she scanned the room, searching for Rachel. There was no sign of her friend in the crowd, and Mary figured Rachel was probably waiting for her boyfriend, Paul, to show up.

Lucy was there, though. And with Dan Telly. They were both locked into a discussion about divinity school.

Dan's brother, Chuck, was dancing with Leigh, and Bob and Sally Hopkins were together, arm in arm, drinking punch and talking to Sheena Stapleton. Watching the two statuesque lifeguards, Mary couldn't decide who was taller, Sheena or Sally.

Outside the beach house, Simon was holding hands with Amy Reese. He couldn't take his eyes off her.

Amy was wearing low-slung bell-bottom jeans and a skimpy white blouse.

A purple crystal dangled from her belly button.

"This will be fun!" Simon insisted.

"I don't know," Amy said doubtfully. "I don't like to fraternize with the help."

"What?" Simon said, stopping in his tracks.

"You know," Amy replied. "A girl's got to remain image-conscious if she's going to be a movie star someday."

"Come on," Simon insisted. "This party is in honor of my sister. Mary isn't the help! She's a lifeguard and a hero."

Amy smiled and kissed Simon on the nose.

"I'll do it for you," she purred. "But only because you're so cute."

They walked a few steps, and then Amy stopped abruptly.

"Yuck!" she said. "It's Paul Tilson."

Simon had never heard the name. He turned and saw a guy with blond hair talking to a girl sitting in a cherry-red BMW convertible. He leaned into the car and kissed her passionately.

"Old boyfriend?" Simon asked.

"No way!" Amy cried. "He used to be

one of the lifeguards around here. Hit on me all last summer, the creep. I heard he got a job at the Valley Fountain Lodge. That girl he's with now looks like one of the regulars there. The Lodge is real swanky and exclusive," Amy continued. "Only the richest of the rich can afford to stay there."

"What's this guy Paul doing here, then?" asked Simon.

Amy shrugged. "I heard he has a girlfriend at Pacific Paradise," she said. "But that can't be her."

The sound of music and laughter wafted out on the cool night air.

"Who cares? Let's party!" Simon said, leading her into the beach house.

Ruthie was breathless when she arrived at the rescue party. It took her so long to get back from Rachel's secret place that she didn't have time to change.

Ruthie didn't feel like celebrating, anyway. She just wanted to find Mary and tell her all she knew about Rachel and her violent boyfriend, Paul.

But Ruthie had a hard time pushing

through the press of people to get to her sister. As she squeezed between two couples, Lucy collared her instead.

"Where have you been?" Lucy demanded. "You missed the call to Dad and Mom this afternoon. I had to make up a story about how you were in the bathtub."

"I was . . . Oh, never mind," Ruthie replied. "I have to talk to Mary."

"Well, she's busy right now," Lucy shot back. "Just sit down here and wait for her to come over."

Sighing, Ruthie plunked down in a chair next to Lucy and her new friend. She rolled her eyes as Lucy and the lifeguard made small talk.

I have to see Mary! she thought.

When it looked like Mary was about to come over and say hello, her boss, Ray Broome, grabbed her hand.

"Over here, Mary," he said, leading her to a small raised platform.

Mary and Ray climbed the three steps and stood together.

"Quiet down, everybody!" Ray Broome called. The noise decreased, and all eyes turned to the makeshift podium.

Ray drew a small jewelry box out of his shirt pocket.

"In honor of your rescue today, I am presenting you with the Pacific Paradise mark of excellence."

He handed the box to Mary, and she opened it. Inside she found an ankle bracelet. It was made of tiny links of gold chain and dozens of little green gemstones.

She recognized it instantly. Sally Hopkins wore three of them around her ankle.

"Congratulations, Mary Camden," Ray Broome said, smiling. "Wear it with pride."

Everyone began to applaud. Flashbulbs snapped as people took pictures.

"How about a few words!" someone yelled.

"I don't know what to say," Mary replied. "Only that this is a real honor. And I thank you."

There were cheers and more clapping.

Ray Broome touched Mary's shoulder. "Mr. and Mrs. Kelly are in my office. They want to thank you personally for saving their daughter."

"Sure," Mary said.

Ray led Mary to his office, and the party continued.

Ruthie waited for nearly an hour for Mary to come back. Finally, Lucy tapped her on the shoulder.

"Come on," she said. "It's past your bedtime."

"But I want to talk to Mary!" Ruthie insisted.

"You can talk to her tomorrow. First thing in the morning if you have to," Lucy replied.

"But—"

"No buts," Lucy shot back. "Mom and Dad made you my responsibility, and it's time to go. Dan has graciously offered to escort the two of us back to the cottage. So let's go."

"Fine!" Ruthie said, throwing up her hands.

But as Lucy and her friend led Ruthie away, the youngest Camden sister couldn't help thinking that leaving the party now—before she got a chance to talk to Mary—was a terrible mistake.

THIRTEEN

Mary awoke late on the morning after the rescue party. She opened her eyes to see a spider crawling down a shimmering thread dangling from the ceiling. The creature twisted in the air, right over Mary's bed.

"Yuck," she cried, pushing the creepy crawler aside. Her cottage was as dreary as ever, but to Mary the whole world had a rosy glow this beautiful Sunday morning.

It's nice to be a hero!

Mary checked her watch. It was a quarter to eleven. She knew she'd better hurry or she would be late for duty, even though she had second shift today. Before she left for the ready room, Mary opened the box and drew out the ankle bracelet. With a rush of pride, she clipped it on. The jewelry tickled her foot—a constant reminder of her heroics the day before.

The ready room was crowded, as usual. Everyone greeted Mary when she came in. Ray Broome handed out the afternoon assignments, then went back to his office for an appointment.

Mary drew Beach 4 again.

"The folks who hang out there will be expecting to see you today," he explained. "Everyone loves a hero! Tomorrow I'll assign you to one of the easy beaches, I promise."

Then Mary went to her locker. She was hoping to run into Rachel. She missed her friend last night. Mary figured Rachel preferred to spend the evening with her boyfriend, and she felt a little hurt.

Rachel could have at least said hello to me. And I could have introduced her to Simon. They haven't met.

Mary lingered as long as she could, hoping to see Rachel. But soon it was time to go to work, and she headed off to Beach 4.

Outside, Mary spotted Paul Tilson. He was leaving Ray Broome's office. Though she didn't like him very much, Mary wanted to ask about Rachel, so she approached him.

"Hey," Mary said casually. "What's up?"

Paul whirled around and glared at her. He looked meaner and nastier than ever.

"What business is it of yours?" he said angrily.

"Sorry," Mary said. "I was just wondering if you've seen Rachel."

"No!" Paul barked. "I haven't. But if you find her first, tell her I was here. Tell her I was looking for her."

Paul pushed past Mary and stalked away.

"You have a nice day, too," Mary muttered softly. "Jerk!"

"Mary," Ray Broome called. He was standing outside. Mary realized he must have witnessed her conversation with Paul Tilson.

"Don't let Paul get to you," Ray Broome said. "He just got some bad news."

"Really?"

Ray nodded. "He came here yesterday, but with all the excitement I couldn't talk with him."

Then Ray yanked the cap off his bald

head and scratched behind his ear.

"Paul came to my office just now and begged me to give him his old job back," Ray explained. "I had to tell him no. I don't know what that kid was thinking!" Ray exclaimed. "He had a good job here and a nice girlfriend, too. But a couple of weeks ago he just up and quit. Left me in a bind, too. I was short one lifeguard."

Ray looked at Mary. "That's why I hired you. To replace Paul. And I sure wasn't going to lose you to hire him back. Not after he quit like that. Not after your rescue yesterday."

Mary blinked. *No wonder Paul was angry with me. I would be angry, too.*

"In fact," Ray added, "I was kind of hoping you'd stay here—full-time, that is."

Mary was surprised. "That's nice, but—"

"It's a great position. Good pay. Good benefits," Ray continued. "I could always use a conscientious lifeguard like you around here!"

"Gee, I—"

"Don't make up your mind yet!" Ray said. "Just think about it."

"Okay."

"One more thing," said Ray. "A fellow is going to pay you a visit today. His name is Keith Rimirez. He runs the *Pacific Paradise Gazette,* a weekly community paper. Keith wants to interview you about the rescue."

"Sure," Mary said, surprised yet again.

"Be careful out there," said Ray with a fatherly wink.

Placing his hat on his head, Ray Broome hurried off. So did Mary. She burst into a run, toward Beach 4 and another day of work.

Mary wasn't at her post an hour when Lucy and Ruthie showed up at Beach 4. Lucy spread out her beach towel and lay back. But Ruthie seemed edgy and couldn't relax.

"I need to talk to you," Ruthie said. "It's really important."

"Well, I can't talk now," Mary explained. "I'm on duty. If I get distracted by conversation, I might miss something. Someone might get hurt."

"But this is real important," Ruthie insisted.

"Couldn't you talk to Lucy about it?"

Ruthie stared at Lucy. "She's distracted, too," Ruthie replied.

Lucy was lost in conversation with Dan Telly. Dan wasn't wearing his lifeguard vest, which meant he was off duty. There were school catalogs and folders spread out on the blanket, and Lucy was writing in a notepad.

"Listen, Ruthie," Mary said. "Let's have dinner tonight—just you and me—and you can tell me what's bothering you."

Ruthie frowned.

"Okay," she said after a pause. "I just hope it's not too late."

Mary smiled as her little sister plopped down on Lucy's beach blanket and tucked her feet in the sand.

Ruthie seemed very upset, but Mary reminded herself that when she was Ruthie's age, every problem was a crisis, every minor setback a tragedy.

"Hello," a voice said.

A cute guy a little older than Mary appeared at her side. He had a dark tan, and his ebony hair was slicked back. The man thrust out his hand.

"My name is Keith Rimirez," he said.

"From the *Pacific Paradise Gazette.*"

Mary smiled and shook his hand. But her eyes never left the surf, which was crowded with swimmers.

"I wonder if I might have a word with you," Keith said. "I wanted to write an article about your rescue yesterday."

Sitting with Dan, Lucy looked over and her ears perked up.

"Wow!" she said. "A newspaper article."

"Friend of yours?" Keith asked, indicating Lucy.

"My sister," Mary replied.

"Lucy Camden," she said, rising from her blanket to shake Keith's hand.

Mary blew her whistle. "Take your football game away from the little kids," she yelled.

A gang of boys waved at her and moved on.

"The interview should only take half an hour or so," Keith said to Mary.

But to his surprise, she shook her head. "I'm really busy," she told him. "Maybe if you come again near the end of my shift."

Keith Rimirez nodded. "I understand.

How about I come back at sunset?"

"Sunset, it is," Mary replied, before rushing off to stop some rough horseplay.

"Maybe you can help," Keith said to Lucy.

Lucy blinked in surprise. "Me?"

"Sure," Keith said. "If I get a little background on Mary, it will save time later."

"That's my cue," Dan said, gathering up the folders and catalogs. "I've got to go, anyway. See you later?"

"It's a date," Lucy replied with a smile.

Keith Rimirez sat down on the blanket next to Lucy. "So where do you and your sisters all come from?" he asked.

"No comment!" Ruthie declared.

"We live in Glenoak," Lucy replied.

"So how do you both feel about your sister's rescue yesterday?"

"Talk to my press agent," Ruthie said.

"We're all really proud," Lucy told the reporter, shooting Ruthie a look. "Mary had the whole family worried for a while, but now she's really putting her life back together."

It was Keith's ears that perked up this time. Unseen by Lucy or Ruthie, Keith

Rimirez reached into his pocket and activated a tiny tape recorder hidden there.

"Was Mary in some kind of trouble?" Keith asked.

Ruthie rolled her eyes. "Loose lips sink ships," she warned.

Lucy's mouth snapped shut. She realized that she had maybe said too much. "Well, not really," Lucy lied. "Just some adolescent stuff. Mary is really cool these days. She's responsible and has a good job."

"I'm out of here," Ruthie said.

She got up and stalked away, hoping for once that Lucy would keep her big mouth shut.

With the tape player recording all that was being said, Keith Rimirez leaned close to Lucy.

"Tell me more," he said.

She did.

"Mary was always athletic," Simon told Keith Rimirez. "That's why she's such a great lifeguard."

After his revealing interview with Lucy Camden, the reporter set out to interview Mary's brother, Simon. Keith Rimirez cornered him at the snack bar, where Simon had been waiting for Amy Reese to meet him.

"Was she into swimming in high school?" the reporter asked.

"Basketball," Simon replied. "Mary was captain of the team. They were the league champs her sophomore and junior years."

"Not senior year?" Rimirez asked.

"Ah, no," Simon said, recalling the trouble Mary and her team got into senior year. "Some stuff happened, and Mary's team didn't make the play-offs."

"Too bad," Keith replied. Inside his pocket, his recorder was taping every word. "Does Mary have a boyfriend?" Keith asked.

"Not now," Simon replied. "But she had lots of boyfriends before. For a while she was dating some older guy—an international airline pilot or something."

Keith Rimirez raised his eyebrow.

"All I mean to say is that Mary was—was popular, that's all," Simon stammered. "She was even engaged once. . . . Or was it twice?"

Rimirez listened intently. His face was bland, but inside, the reporter was laughing. He knew he had tapped into a gold mine of information here. Even though the Camden siblings were trying to be discreet, the reporter knew now that Mary had a hidden past. He was determined to find out what it was—and print the facts in the next edition.

Keith Rimirez loved a scoop. And the bigger the secret, the better the scoop.

"Hi," Amy Reese said as she sauntered up to the pair.

"I'm glad you're here!" Simon cried, jumping to his feet. "I've got to go, Mr. Rimirez. Sorry."

"Don't worry about it," Keith Rimirez replied. "I've got plenty of information."

"But you didn't take any notes," said Simon.

Keith smiled. "I have a good memory," he replied.

It was nearly sunset when Keith Rimirez arrived back at Beach 4 to interview Mary.

The beach was nearly empty now, and no one was in the water. Mary climbed down from her tall lifeguard chair and sat next to Keith Rimirez in the sand.

As Keith asked her a bunch of questions,

Mary answered them as best she could. She told him how much she liked working at Pacific Paradise. How much she liked the people there.

Then Keith asked Mary to tell him about the rescue of Debbie Kelly, from her point of view.

As Mary launched into her story, she noticed Rachel Glover on the far side of the beach, near the rocks. Rachel was wearing her baggy sweatpants and a loose-fitting, long-sleeve shirt despite the afternoon heat.

Rachel didn't seem to notice Mary. Mary wanted to run over and ask the girl where she'd been for the last twenty-four hours, but Keith distracted Mary with another question.

She noticed a little while later that Rachel walked to the water. Dipping her foot into the surf, the girl pulled her sweatpants up over her knees and waded in.

"You come from Glenoak, right?" Keith asked.

Mary nodded.

"What's it like there?"

As the sun dipped lower and lower,

Keith Rimirez continued his interview. The beach cleared completely except for Rachel, who waded into deeper water.

"No boyfriend?" Keith asked.

"Not now," Mary replied. "But I'm hopeful."

"I heard that you really liked sports in high school," Keith continued.

Mary told the reporter about her athletic career, ending with the story of the knee injury that forced her to sit out half a season.

Finally, there was a lag in the conversation, and Mary scanned the beach. She saw Rachel's blanket and stuff, still lying on the sand. Then her eyes scanned the water.

Mary's heart skipped a beat when she noticed that there was no sign of Rachel Glover.

"Oh, no," Mary groaned.

"What?" asked Keith.

Mary leaped to her feet and scanned the beach again. She squinted into the sun in an effort to locate her friend.

Frightened now, Mary ran over to Rachel's blanket. Her towel was there, and so was the girl's wallet. Mary opened it and saw a little bit of money and Rachel's Pacific Paradise employee card.

Mary had hoped that Rachel simply wandered off, forgetting her beach towel. But Mary knew that there was no way Rachel would forget her wallet.

Mary ran back to her lifeguard station and lifted the walkie-talkie.

"Mayday! Mayday!" she said. "Swimmer in the water on Beach 4."

Then Mary ran to the edge of the water and scanned the horizon again, hoping.

Keith Rimirez returned to his office well after sunset. Now he had two last-minute stories to write for tomorrow's edition.

One about the apparent disappearance and possible drowning of Rachel Glover.

The other about the real Mary Camden, the "hero" lifeguard who should have been watching the beach when Rachel turned up missing.

Keith sat in front of his computer terminal for a moment. Then he reached for the phone.

He had to call a friend. A fellow journalist who lived and worked in Glenoak.

Even if Mary's juvenile record were sealed, his crime reporter friend might have heard something.

Keith Rimirez was determined to learn just what kind of trouble Mary had gotten herself into while she was still in high school.

FOURTEEN

As night fell, the beaches at Pacific Paradise were illuminated by brilliant searchlights. Flashing lights from a dozen emergency vehicles tinted the sand red. Police officers, firefighters, and ambulance crews walked the beach and searched the surrounding blocks, looking for any sign of the missing girl.

Off the coast, beyond the buoys that marked the end of the swimming area, Coast Guard patrol boats cut through the black water. Boat crews called out to one another with bullhorns as searchlights stabbed the darkness.

The roar of a helicopter shook the trees

as a Coast Guard rescue aircraft dropped out of the night sky. It circled the beach, the propellers kicking up sand. Then the helicopter turned and moved out to sea and out of sight.

On the shoreline, lifeguards from all around the county scoured Beach 4.

They found no body, which gave everyone hope.

"Maybe she got caught by the tide and was carried out to sea," Ray Broome said hopefully. "Like that little girl a few years ago . . ."

"We have a Coast Guard cutter out there now," Captain Fletcher said. "If she's there, we'll find her."

By Ray's side stood Mary Camden. Her face was pale, her eyes wide. The cool night air made her shiver in her swimsuit, but Mary refused to waste time changing her clothes. Her friend Rachel was gone—and it was her fault.

A Coast Guard sailor ran across the beach.

"Sir," the man said to Captain Fletcher. "We have two more boats ready to search the coast."

"I've got to go, Ray," Captain Fletcher declared. "I'm going to make a run of the coast in case the body—"

Captain Fletcher saw Mary wince.

"—in case the girl washed ashore somewhere."

"Let me go with you," Mary pleaded.

Captain Fletcher shook his head. "I can't see how it would help."

"I can help," Mary insisted. "I have to. I'm ready to do anything."

Captain Fletcher's eyes locked with Mary's.

"Okay," he said. "Let's go. I'll get you back to this beach by midnight. After that, the search will end until morning."

Mary walked off with Captain Fletcher without meeting Ray Broome's accusing stare.

In truth, Mary was happy to get away. Happy to escape the stares of other lifeguards at Pacific Paradise.

Worst of all was the way Ray Broome looked at her. Mary knew he was blaming her.

Why not? thought Mary bitterly. *It is my fault.*

* * *

Lucy had just stepped out of the shower when Dan Telly knocked on the door of the cottage.

"Sorry to bother you, Lucy," Dan said. He was wearing his lifeguard outfit. "I just came by to see how you were. We're on double duty because of the accident, and I can only stay a minute."

"What happened?" Lucy cried, suddenly worried.

Ruthie, who had been waiting for hours to see Mary, ran to the door. Simon was still in his shower, getting ready for his date with Amy.

"I was afraid that you hadn't heard," Dan said, frowning. "That's why I stopped by."

"Oh, no," Ruthie said, fearful that it was bad news about Rachel.

"Rachel Glover disappeared in the ocean this afternoon," Dan explained. "We think she got caught up in the tide near the rocks. Maybe she got swept out to sea and is still alive, or maybe . . ."

His voice trailed off.

"I don't understand," Lucy cried. "That was Mary's station. Mary was watching that beach!"

Dan nodded. "Your sister was on duty when it happened. Claimed she didn't see a thing."

Lucy gasped.

"I've got to go," Dan said, hurrying away.

"This is terrible!" Lucy said, sinking into a chair. Ruthie sat down next to her but said nothing.

Maybe this isn't an accident, Ruthie thought. *Maybe Paul did something terrible to Rachel.*

Ruthie knew she just had to talk to Mary as soon as she could.

"What's going on?" a freshly dressed Simon asked as he entered the room.

Lucy told him what happened.

"I'm going down to the beach to find Mary!" he declared.

"Wait!" Lucy called. "I'm going with you."

"So am I!" Ruthie cried.

Together, they rushed into the night.

Down at the beach, they could see the flashing lights and the searchlights on the water. But as they approached a line of emergency vehicles, a policeman stopped them.

"Nobody's permitted beyond this point but emergency personnel," he informed them. "You have to go back."

"But we need to see Mary Camden!" Lucy insisted. "She's our sister."

The look on the cop's face told them he recognized the name.

"Your sister Mary is busy right now," he said tersely. "I'm sure the Coast Guard has a lot of questions to ask her."

"But we—"

The policeman cut Simon off. "You'd better go. Right now."

"What do we do?" Lucy said as they headed back to the cottage.

"We do nothing until we talk to Mary," Simon replied. "We need to hear her side of the story. Do you know where she's staying?"

"She refused to tell me," Lucy replied.

Ruthie said nothing, which was unusual. Unfortunately Lucy and Simon were too frantic to notice their sister's odd behavior.

"You know what we're supposed to do, don't you?" Lucy said.

"We are not calling Mom and Dad," Simon replied. "Not until we talk to Mary."

Lucy nodded. She knew Simon was right. But it was hard. Without the guidance of their parents, they were on their own.

So this is what it's like to be an adult, Lucy thought. *I don't think I like it very much.*

It was nearly midnight when the Coast Guard boat carrying Mary and Captain Fletcher slid onto the sand at Beach 4.

To Mary's surprise, the beach was deserted.

"The search is over until first light," Captain Fletcher told her.

"Can't we make another run up the coast?" Mary pleaded.

"Look," the captain replied. "Be here at six tomorrow morning and we'll go out on the search together."

Mary nodded, her heart sinking.

"The best thing you can do is get some sleep," Captain Fletcher said.

He waved his arm and the sailor backed the flat-bottomed boat away from the shore. With a roar of its engines, the boat vanished in the darkness.

I have to do something, Mary thought.

Instead of going back to her cottage, Mary scanned the dark beach. Finally, she decided to walk the length of Pacific Paradise one last time.

Maybe there was still hope.

At exactly six o'clock, an exhausted Mary arrived on Beach 4. Some of the lifeguards were already assembled on the beach, including Bob and Sally Hopkins and Sheena Stapleton. They looked tired and disheveled. They were dressed in yesterday's clothes, as if they had been up most of the night, too.

Ray Broome was also there. He was locked in an animated conversation with a pudgy man in a gray suit. The man waved a newspaper in Ray's face.

"What's going on?" Mary asked Sheena.

The girl shrugged. "Someone said that guy in the suit is from the insurance company. He got here a few minutes ago, shaking today's edition of the *Pacific Paradise Gazette* in Ray's face. I haven't seen the paper yet," Sheena said. "But there must be a story about Rachel's disappearance on the front page."

Mary's heart skipped a beat. She'd forgotten that Keith Rimirez had been there when she discovered Rachel was missing. He must have written about it.

Mary watched as the man in the suit threw the paper at Ray Broome's feet and stormed off. He climbed into a black BMW and drove away.

Ray bent down and lifted the newspaper out of the sand. He looked at the front page and shook his head. Then he saw Mary.

She ran over.

"Explain this!" Ray said, displaying the front page.

Mary gasped when she saw the headline. There was a huge picture of her there, too—her high school yearbook photo. And in big, bold letters the front page read:

"HEROIC" LIFEGUARD'S SHADY PAST

TRASHED HS GYM AFTER

SCHOOL SUSPENSION OF TEAM

Mary covered her mouth with her hand and shook her head numbly.

"You didn't tell me you were a vandal. That you had a criminal record!" Ray shouted, loud enough for everyone to hear.

"I—I wasn't trying to hide anything,"

Mary stammered. "It's all there, on my application!"

"That's not the point!" Ray shouted. "You didn't tell me."

"Ray! Ray!" Leigh Rogers cried as she raced across the sand. Puffing after the effort, she could barely get out the words.

"Last night . . . someone . . . someone broke into the Surf Shop," she gasped. "The lockers, too. The ready room has been burglarized!"

The police wasted no time and grabbed Mary minutes after they arrived. A policeman took Mary into Ray Broome's office and began to grill her right in front of her boss.

"Captain Fletcher tells us he dropped you off last night at about midnight," the officer said. "What did you do after that?"

"I searched for Rachel," Mary replied.

"So you have nobody to vouch for your whereabouts between 1 and 5 A.M.?"

"No," Mary replied. "I was alone. What difference does it make?"

The policeman stared down at Mary.

"Ms. Camden," he said sternly. "Last night between 1 and 5 A.M. someone broke into the Surf Shop and stole clothing. Then someone broke into the ready room and, using a crowbar, pried open the lockers and stole money and personal items from them, too. Only one locker was undisturbed, Ms. Camden," the policeman told her.

"That locker belongs to you."

FIFTEEN

Lucy ran to the cottage door and yanked it open before the person could knock twice. To her surprise, Mary stood on the veranda, clutching her suitcase.

Her eyes were red from crying, and she ran into her sister's arms.

"He fired me," Mary sobbed. "Ray fired me."

Lucy hugged her sister as Simon and Ruthie appeared.

"We couldn't find you anywhere," Simon told Mary. "The police wouldn't let anyone near the beach last night or all day."

"We saw the paper," Lucy said. "That Rimirez is a real creep! Is that why you were fired?"

"It wasn't the paper," Mary said. "Well, maybe it was. But there was also a burglary, and I got blamed. The police interrogated me all afternoon. Then Ray gave me an hour to pack up my stuff and leave my cottage."

"What happened?" said Lucy.

"Last night someone robbed the Surf Shop and jimmied the lockers in the ready room, too," Mary explained. "Ray Broome blamed me. He said I already had a criminal record. Even after the police said they didn't have any evidence, Ray said he wanted me gone."

Mary shook her head. "I even let the police search my cottage for the stolen items. Of course they found nothing. But Ray fired me, anyway. I'm sure he blames me for Rachel. Everybody does. And they're right!"

Mary dropped her suitcase and leaned against Lucy. Simon took her hand and led her to the living room.

"First Rachel. Now this," Mary said, frowning. "How could I be so stupid? It's all my fault."

"Maybe it isn't."

Mary looked at Ruthie.

"Maybe it isn't your fault," Ruthie insisted. "Maybe none of this is your fault."

"What are you getting at?" Mary demanded.

Ruthie suddenly seemed reluctant to speak. "Maybe Mary and I should talk alone," she said.

"It's too late for secrets now," Mary replied.

"But it's about Rachel," cried Ruthie.

"Even secrets about Rachel," Mary said. "She can't be hurt. Not now."

Ruthie lowered her eyes. "Maybe I shouldn't say anything. I don't have all the facts. And maybe it's none of our business, anyway."

Mary gripped Ruthie's arms. "You're wrong, Ruthie. It *is* our business. If you know something. Something that can help Rachel or help us find Rachel, you've got to tell," Mary told her. "If people know bad things are happening, it's their duty to tell someone they trust."

A tear rolled down Ruthie's cheek, and she told them everything. About Paul and Rachel in the Surf Shop and what she saw at the cove later on. When Ruthie was finished, they sat in silence for a long time.

Finally, Mary spoke. "Ruthie is going to lead me to this secret cove," she announced. "While Simon goes over to the Valley Fountain Lodge to have a talk with Paul Tilson. Maybe he knows what happened to Rachel."

"What about me?" Lucy asked.

"You have the most dangerous job of us all," Mary told her. "You are going to call Mom and Dad and tell them everything."

"You can't be serious!" Lucy cried.

"I am," Mary insisted. "We have to practice what we preach. I told Ruthie that if she knew about something bad, she should tell someone she trusts. Now I'm going to take my own advice. We're going to tell Mom and Dad everything. Period."

Lucy, Simon, and Ruthie nodded. They knew Mary was right. Then Simon got the keys to the van while Mary hunted up a flashlight. Lucy sat down and lifted the phone.

"Don't call until we're gone," Mary said. "That way Dad can't order us to stay in the cottage and wait three hours for him to drive here."

"Good idea!" Simon said.

When everyone was gone, Lucy stared at the telephone for a long time. Then, hands shaking, she picked up the receiver and dialed.

Simon walked down a long hotel corridor until he reached room 59. He rechecked the number, then paused in front of the door for a moment, listening. Finally, Simon knocked. He heard a muffled sound from behind the door and knocked again—this time harder.

The door opened an inch or two. An unfamiliar face peered through the crack. A guy about Paul's age, with a shaved head, glared at Simon.

"I'm looking for Paul Tilson," Simon said evenly.

"He isn't here," the guy replied, starting to close the door again.

But Simon instantly threw his weight against the barrier and pushed his way into the room.

"Hey, man!" the other guy cried, jumping aside. Simon stepped into the tiny room and looked around.

"See!" the other guy said. "I told you Paul wasn't here."

"Who are you?" Simon demanded.

"I'm Darren, Paul's roommate," the man replied nervously. "Or I was. Look, man, if Paul hit on your girlfriend or something, don't take it personally. Paul hits on all the girls. That's just his style."

"Do you know Rachel Glover?" Simon asked. "Paul's girlfriend?"

"I know her," Darren replied. "But I didn't think she was his girlfriend anymore. Paul told me he dumped her. Paul said why would he want Rachel when he could have his pick of the rich girls staying here?"

"Where is he!" Simon demanded, running out of patience.

Darren shrugged. "How should I know? Paul got fired today. He had to move out."

"Fired! Why?"

"The management caught him with the much younger daughter of a rich guest," Darren said. "Somebody complained and Paul got the boot. The boss gave him an hour to pack his things and get out. I haven't seen him since."

"What about the cove?" Simon said. "You do know about the cove. Right?"

"Sure," Darren replied. "Sometimes Paul takes his girlfriends there to be alone. He lived there for a while. Him and Rachel. When they first got to California. Before they found jobs."

Then Darren snapped his fingers. "Hey, I remember! Paul did say something about spending one last night at the cove before moving on to Hollywood! Said he had something to take care of first—before he could start his new life in Los Angeles."

Before Darren could say another word, Simon was gone.

He ran down the corridor and out to the parking lot. Simon started the engine and raced his van through the security gate at the Valley Fountain Lodge without slowing down.

Simon's mind raged.

Mary might be in danger! He knew he had to warn her—somehow—that Paul Tilson was on his way to the cove or was there already!

It was a clear night with a full moon, but even with a flashlight the trek along the cliffs was difficult and dangerous.

Though Ruthie knew the way to the cove, it was Mary who took the lead, testing each ledge and rock to see if it could hold their weight.

Even before they could see the cove, Mary and Ruthie heard voices. The sound echoed off the rocks.

"That's Rachel's voice," Ruthie hissed.

"How much farther?" Mary asked.

"It's just down there, to the right," Ruthie told her. "You can see the path down to the cove. It starts right there."

Even over the roar of the pounding surf, they could hear shouting.

"She's not alone," Ruthie said.

Mary turned and knelt down. She handed Ruthie the flashlight, then gripped her shoulders.

"Ruthie, listen to me," Mary said, her voice tense. "I want you to start back. Just follow the path until you get to Beach 4, then use the emergency box at my lifeguard station to call the police."

"What are you going to do?"

Ruthie's face was pale in the moonlight, her features pinched with fear.

"I have to go down there," Mary said. "To rescue Rachel."

"You can't!" Ruthie cried. "He might hurt you."

"Paul is not going to hurt me," Mary insisted. "I'm just going to go down there and take Rachel back with me, that's all. But in case something goes wrong, I want the police to know what's happened. So you have to tell them. Okay?"

Ruthie nodded, a tear welling up in her eye.

"Come here," Mary said, holding her little sister close. "No matter what, remember that I love you."

Ruthie nodded, too afraid to speak because she was sure she'd cry.

"You are so brave!" Mary said. "Now go!"

Mary watched Ruthie climb up the path. Then, from below, she heard Paul's angry voice. Then Rachel screamed.

Mary jumped to her feet and ran along the rocky path that led down to the cove.

"Why did you come here?" Paul Tilson screamed. "Are you trying to hide from me? Pretend you're dead?"

Rachel quaked as her boyfriend screamed at her.

"Your little act might fool that moron Ray and his stupid lifeguards, but I knew I would find you hiding here!"

Paul's eyes were bright from the reflection of the tiny fire Rachel had started to keep warm.

"Don't be angry," Rachel sobbed. "I just wanted to get away. Start a new life. I didn't want to get you into trouble, so I just ran away. . . . I promise I won't tell anyone what you did to me if you just leave me alone."

But Paul reached out and grabbed Rachel's arm. He pulled her close, then threw her to the ground. The girl scrambled along the flat, slippery rock to get away from him.

Still angry, Paul kicked the fire. A cloud of burning cinders exploded like fireworks.

"I never should have brought you to California!" Paul cried. "You've been holding me back ever since we got here."

"What did I do?" Rachel asked. "I loved you, that's all. I wanted the best for you, even when you hurt me for no reason."

"That's a lie!" Paul shouted. "Everything was going great until my stupid roommate Darren told Megan Crawford I had a girlfriend at Pacific Paradise!"

Rachel's eyes filled with tears. She never knew Paul had another girlfriend.

"Megan was going to take me to Hollywood. Introduce me to people. Important people!" Paul screamed. "Until she found out about you."

Paul crouched down on his heels and gripped his head in his hands.

"Megan complained to the management of the resort, and they fired me!" Paul yelled. "Now I don't even have a job!"

"You . . . you don't need a job, Paul," Rachel said. "Look!"

She got up and ran to her backpack. She pulled out clothes and threw them aside. Then she reached deep inside.

"I have money, Paul!" she said, showing him a wad of bills. "Enough for you to go to Hollywood if you want to. Take it and leave me alone!"

Paul rushed forward and stood over Rachel, fists clenched, ready to strike.

"Don't touch her!" Mary Camden cried.

Paul whirled around to see Mary standing behind him, legs braced, arms raised and ready to defend herself.

"Well, well. The girl who took my job," Paul said with an evil smirk.

Paul threw himself at Mary, his fist raised to strike her.

"No!" Rachel screamed.

Rachel jumped to her feet and threw herself at Paul to protect Mary. They struggled for a moment, then Paul grabbed Rachel's arms and shook her.

"Get away from me," he shouted, pushing her across the ledge. Rachel stumbled backward, then slipped on the wet rock.

With a shrill scream, Rachel plunged off the edge of the boulder and into the pounding surf twenty feet below.

Without a moment's hesitation, Mary ran to the edge of the rocky cliff and pushed Paul Tilson aside. He tried to hit her, but Mary shoved her elbow into his ribs and he buckled over.

Then she extended her arms above her head and dived down, down into the dark water.

SIXTEEN

Mary felt a sharp jolt as she struck the waves. Her head spun for a moment as she plunged deep down to touch the rocks. Kicking hard, Mary shot to the surface again.

When her head poked above water, Mary could hear a beating sound. It got louder and louder.

Suddenly a brilliant arc of light pierced the night and illuminated the crashing surf. In the spotlight, Mary could see Rachel bobbing on the waves. She wasn't moving.

With long, powerful strokes, Mary swam to Rachel's side and held her head above the surface of the water so she could breathe. Mary felt something warm on the back of Rachel's head. Blood. The girl had struck her head on a rock.

Above the noise of the waves, Rachel moaned.

"Hold on," Mary cried. "Help is on the way."

Looking up, Mary saw a Coast Guard helicopter hovering over her head. The chopper swung away from the ledge and Mary could see people inside the open door—Captain Fletcher and Ray Broome among them.

A rope dropped out of the helicopter door, and someone in black scuba gear rappelled down to splash into the water close to Mary.

A head covered with a breathing mask and goggles popped out of the water beside Mary. Strong hands fastened a harness around Rachel's waist, then Mary's.

Seconds later, Mary found herself being hauled out of the water, dangling from a long rope. The entire area around the cove was illuminated. There were people on the rocks—police and a rescue crew.

One policeman had Paul Tilson face-down on the flat rock. He put handcuffs on

Paul's wrists, then dragged him to his feet again.

Then hands reached out and pulled Mary inside the helicopter. The interior was lit with scarlet lights. Mary struggled out of the harness and rushed to Rachel's side. A Coast Guard midshipman and a paramedic were already working on the girl.

"She'll be all right, I'm sure of it," Captain Fletcher said as he draped a blanket over Mary's shivering shoulders.

Then the man smiled. "That was quite a rescue," he said, patting Mary's arm.

Mary tried to smile, but the interior of the helicopter suddenly seemed to spin. She lay back and closed her eyes and let the vibration of the helicopter rock her to sleep.

"After Rachel Glover woke up at the hospital, she confessed to the police that she'd faked her own death and robbed the Surf Shop," Reverend Camden explained. "She was afraid of Paul, of what he would do to her. But she was also afraid to lose him. Rachel told the detective who talked to her that she had lost everyone whom she loved and Paul was all she had left. That's why she stayed with him so long. Rachel said that it wasn't until she met Mary that she had the courage to try to escape her abusive boyfriend."

"How did she get the bruises Ruthie saw?" Mary asked.

"During the interview, Rachel admitted to the police that Paul had hit her that day in the Surf Shop. She also told them that he'd hit her before."

Reverend Camden paused.

He was sitting with Mary, Ruthie, Simon, and Lucy in the living room of Dr. Napier's cottage. He had just come from the hospital. Outside, the sun was just starting to rise.

"How is Rachel?" Mary asked.

"The doctor said she'll be fine," Reverend Camden replied. "Her head injury looked much worse than it was."

"Thank God," Mary said.

"Rachel was more concerned about what happened to you," Reverend Camden said. "She wanted me to tell you she was sorry she got you in trouble. She said she wasn't thinking straight."

Mary shrugged. "It's over now. That's all that matters."

"Rachel said she needed money to get away, which was why she robbed the lockers. She left your locker alone because she didn't want to steal from you." Reverend Camden sighed. "I guess she never thought about the fact that it would make you look guilty."

"Is she going to be arrested?" Lucy asked.

Reverend Camden shook his head. "Ray Broome refused to press charges. But Paul Tilson was arrested and charged with assault and battery. He's in a lot of trouble right now."

"How do the police know what happened?" Mary asked. "I didn't make a statement."

"They will ask you for one eventually," Reverend Camden explained. "Meanwhile, the Coast Guard provided a picture of Paul shoving Rachel over the ledge to the local police."

"Huh?" Mary grunted.

"It's called FLIR," Reverend Camden said. "Forward-looking infrared. They taped Paul, Rachel, and you on that ledge as they approached, using night-vision equipment."

Reverend Camden sighed again. "They say a picture is worth a thousand words, and they got a clear image of Paul hurting Rachel and pushing her over the ledge, too."

"Good," said Simon.

Mary smiled. "But who arranged my rescue?"

Reverend Camden chuckled. "Let's just say it was a group effort," he said.

"When I called Dad," Lucy explained, "he ordered me to call the police. I did, and just as a squad car arrived here, so did Simon."

"I told the police what Darren told me," Simon continued. "About Paul and the cove. About how you were on your way there to investigate and how I thought Paul might hurt you."

"And I just got to the emergency phone at Beach 4 when about a gazillion police cars showed up," Ruthie added.

"Which one of you thought Rachel might be alive and hiding at the cove?" Reverend Camden asked.

"Not me," said Mary. "First I thought she drowned. Then I suspected Paul Tilson had done something to her."

"Not me," Lucy said. "I didn't know what was going on, to be honest."

"Me neither," Simon said. "I was just worried about Mary."

"And what about you, Ruthie?" Reverend Camden asked.

"I knew that Mary was too responsible a lifeguard to let anyone get hurt on her watch," Ruthie explained. "So I knew that Rachel didn't drown. And because I knew that Paul Tilson wasn't around when Rachel vanished, I didn't suspect foul play, either. I guess I figured Rachel wanted to get lost, and the cove was the best place to do it."

"Good work, Ruthie. I'm impressed," said the reverend. "And I'm also impressed that each of you acted responsibly, even without your mom or me here to guide you. It looks like we've got a *few* heroes in our family."

Everyone hugged, and some of the tension of the night before evaporated.

"What's going to happen to Rachel?" Mary asked.

"She's going to stay in the hospital for a day or two, and then she's coming to Glenoak," said Reverend Camden.

Mary was surprised.

"I've had a long talk with Reverend and Mrs. Chappelle," he explained. "It turns out that Rachel has been lying about her age. She's only sixteen, and she needs a guardian. The Chappelles have agreed to take her in."

"That's great," Lucy said. "Maybe we can see her again."

Suddenly Lucy blinked and rubbed her throat. "I feel a little weak," she moaned.

"We all do," Simon said. "We haven't had much sleep."

"Wait a minute," Reverend Camden said, his face full of concern.

"What?" Lucy demanded.

Reverend Camden placed his palm on Lucy's forehead. "You feel hot, and your skin is flushed." Reverend Camden frowned. "It seems that Dr. Napier's plan was faulty," he said.

"Huh?"

"It looks to me, my darling, darling daughter, like you might have caught strep throat after all!"